The Curse of the Black Dragon

Melissa Saari

Whimsical Publications, LLC

Florida

The Curse of the Black Dragon is a work of fiction. Names, characters, and incidents are the products of the author's imagination and are either fictitious or are used fictitiously. Any resemblance to actual events or persons, living or dead, is entirely coincidental.

To purchase the authorized electronic edition of *The Curse of the Black Dragon*, visit www.whimsicalpublications.com

Cover art by Shyanne England
Editing by Brieanna Robertson

ISBN-13: 978-1-63495-022-0

Published by
Whimsical Publications, LLC
Florida

The lava heating the plateau, agitated by the storms, began to simmer and boil within her to such an extent that she could no longer control the pressure inside. As lava began to pour out of her knee, rolling across the plateau towards the eagle's nest, the eagle screamed and flew away in panic, abandoning the eggs to save herself.

The lava surrounded the driftwood, and at first smoke, then flames, lifted into the air. She cried out in fear as she hemorrhaged, realizing the danger the eggs were in.

Ilmatar knew her only hope was to extinguish the fire in the sea, protecting the eggs with her powers. She summoned all her divine power and cast a protective ward around the eggs. Then she lowered her massive leg into the ocean so the cold water would cool the eggs and preserve them.

Huge waves thundered in all directions, cresting and breaking from their excessive height and rolling away toward the land. These waves were broken up by the powerful winds of the storm pressing against her.

As her leg descended, bubbles of lava struck the water, sending plumes of steam hissing into the air. The eggs descended, protected by the nest, the thick bed of trees burning from the bottom up, heating the eggs slowly, but still protecting them with the branches that had yet to catch fire.

Ilmatar hoped she had enough time as her leg continued to descend, but her large body took significant time to move at all in the gravity of this planet, time she could not afford as the flames licked ever higher, threatening the eggs with a fiery demise. As her leg descended, she lowered her head as well, so that she could observe the eggs when they landed in the water.

The flaming nest struck the water and broke apart, sending the eggs flying into the air momentarily before spinning back to the sea.

The shock of the turbulent seawater on the hot eggs was more force than her protection ward could absorb. Before her eyes, the sacred eggs shattered into thousands of pieces and disappeared into the ocean as her green eyes sunk beneath the water, hot tears mixing with the seawater and warming her cheeks as she slowly submerged.

The protection ward she had cast was stronger than she thought, for when she looked underwater, she saw the shards of the eggs floating down gently, lines of bubbles floating to the surface. It was a magical sight, but meaningless if the eggs were destroyed.

The protection ward began to sparkle even brighter, collecting magic from the power-filled ocean and increasing.

Ilmatar continued to gaze in amazement as her ward began to pull the many shards of the eggs together into one big egg, more powerful than the ones before it. The surface was all different colors, a majestic patchwork of shards, and the newly formed egg was almost as big as the nest that had carried it. Ilmatar realized this would become a splendid god.

A deep blue glow surrounded the new egg, pulsating like a heartbeat. It grew faster until the throbbing pulse under the waves became a thunderous pounding, as the intensity of the magic grew stronger.

The deep blue transformed to a bright blue, and finally a spectacular white, before the entire egg burst apart and her new baby was hatched into the ocean.

Ilmatar stared in wonder. This new baby was a mixture of sea and sky, a powerful force even as an infant. Almost like a whale, this great ocean creature was massive even at birth. She had small wings, which Ilmatar knew would grow longer in time, and a long flowing tail laced with row after row of colors.

Sea women with long flowing tails and lovely green hair surrounded Ilmatar, swimming in circles. "We are the Nakki," said several of them. "We shall protect you."

Ilmatar stared at this god before her, reaching out to hold her baby. As she did so, a name rang clear in her mind, and she who he was beyond a shadow of a doubt.

"Come here, Loviatar!" The young god recognized her name immediately and turned to her mother with wide eyes.

As the young god reached back for her mother, long, twisting billows of thick black ink surrounded the newly hatched baby and dragged her away, leaving her mother to wail in grief for her stolen child. Being so devoted to compassion and nurturing, she couldn't save her child as a goddess. She knew she needed her brother Ukko's help, far up in the nebula, and his name escaped her lips again and again.

Acknowledgements

As always, I'd like to thank my editors, Janet Durbin and Brieanna Robertson, from Whimsical Publications, without whom my books would likely never see the light of day. I thank them from the bottom of my heart.

I'd also like to deliver huge thanks and endless praise to the many fans that are making the first book in the series, *Curse of the Lion People*, a huge success.

Also by
Melissa Saari

The Red Satin Shoes
Blue Satin Diary

Curse of the Lion People

Mystic Lake (coming soon)

The Legend of the Pirate Queen (coming soon)

This book is dedicated to my sister Millie Kish,
who always believes in me.

"Thy founder was the Lord of Hosts,
Who made the earth and swelling sea;
And while their strong foundations stand,
Thy name men's wonder shall command."

From "Song of a Finlandian Country Girl, in the original Finnish, with a literal translation."

"Here under the North Star is our homeland now.
But there, beyond the stars, we will get another home.
Here, like a flower, we have a short time.
There the joy is endless like the angels.
Here, the heart sighs and eyes are filled with tears.
There, the heart is happy and the eyes are showing the joy.
On the wings of hope fly over there, my little heart.
Because there is my homeland and I want to go there."

Traditional Finnish funeral song, "Täällä Pohjantähden Alla"

"Even though you are playful,
Even though you are sulky,
Even when I spoil you,
You look at me and I see your sweetness."

Traditional Finnish lullaby

Chapter One

In the Sky Kingdom above the great world of Santara, the nebula, a vast scintillating cloud of gas, bloomed and swirled for millions of miles on every side of the great Sky Gods.

Two of the Sky Gods living in the nebula were a goddess named Ilmatar and her stormy older brother, a god named Ukko. Ilmatar was about one hundred feet tall, and her hair swirled through the billows of gas, where stray balls of electricity tickled, making her great scalp tingle with the free energy.

The nebula surrounding Santara was turbulent and full of powerful forces. Although the nebula was stormy, Ilmatar was benevolent and peaceful, a generous provider to the people living on the various planets in her arm of the nebula—like the clear sky, calm and warmth-giving. Her limbs were bright blue, yet strong enough to repel any threat. Her eyes were as green as the seaweed in the ocean.

As Ilmatar stared down from the Sky Kingdom to Santara, she felt a deep yearning to be on the surface of the planet with the welcoming ocean, and forsake her beautiful home in the sky.

Far below her, on the land, the goddess could hear music played on harps, and the melodies pulled her in like a spell. Deep inside she desired to hear the music better, to get close enough to the surface that she could dance with them. But the surface of the planet was not her domain. Her place was in the Eastern Sky Kingdom, guarding the planets that bore life in her wing the nebula, a place with lots of blue gas that suited her peaceful personality.

This Southern Wing of the nebula, full of hot yellow gas, and often red and orange jets too, where Santara floated, was Ukko's realm and sometimes he would get jealous of her spending too much time in his domain.

Ilmatar preferred her own domain, where brilliant purple gas surrounded planets like Tulare and Orsako, and blue gas protected younger planets still emerging. Lava running within her veins gave life and heat to the people she nurtured, and her rewards were many.

Ilmatar refused to give another thought to the fact that she was outside of her realm, however. The call of Santara was too much for her to ignore.

Her generous nature stimulated, she breathed, "Oh, how I wish to bring life here! I long to swim through the warm oceans and enrich this planet!"

She never could get used to Ukko's love of lightning and thunder, chaos and energy, but he adored the lightning that flashed between the gas clouds. He fed off that energy, surrounding his thick muscular body with electricity, and sending it out from his lighting rod to shoot thunderbolts at creatures that displeased him.

His hair was silver white, glistening with static, swinging and twisting through the nebula for hundreds of miles, for Ukko was a giant sky god from the early days.

His armor sparkled with magnetism, a powerful shield that deterred even the strongest foes. Blue and green tails of fire tangled across the surface and made his armor shimmer. When there was danger in the Southern wing from a passing demon or a nearby lightning cloud, it was always up to Ukko to protect the fragile planets floating through the clouds of dust.

Ilmatar detected her brother's presence as waves of electricity floated past her. A delicate display of ocean waves played out across the nebula in electric ripples. Ilmatar giggled at Ukko's dance, mesmerized by his artwork.

"The ocean!" she said aloud.

"Does this please you, my sister? Have you fallen in love with the ocean?"

Ilmatar smiled brightly as she saw her powerful brother approach through the nebula.

"Sweet sister, please tell me, what were you talking about just now?"

No doubt crossed Ilmatar's mind, so she missed his sarcasm.

"Oh, dear brother, I want to visit Santara. I want to swim in the ocean and bring life to this planet."

"I have always protected you and entertained you, even though your place is in another arm of the nebula. I have built your magnificent palace, and protected it from danger many times. But still you have abandoned your planets, and come here to stare at a planet in my domain. Was my show not pleasing enough for you? Why do you insist on staring at my planet?"

"Oh, that was pleasing, but the music of the harps is even more pleasing. I want to get closer so I can hear it better! Please, brother, just allow me that much!"

Ukko's face crackled as his temper flared. "What are you talking about, sister? You can't do that!" A bolt of lightning shot from his face and struck a passing asteroid, blasting it to dust.

"I just care so much for these people. Why are you getting so worked up about it? You're supposed to care for these people too! They're in your domain, after all!"

"You are too compassionate, little sister! Your compassion will get the better of you!" Ukko was not calming down.

"How dare you insult my compassion? I love all the people, no matter which planet they're on!"

"We are gods and goddesses. When they ask for rain, I give them rain. That way their crops grow. If I gave them too much water, the crops would be flooded."

Ilmatar was confused by Ukko's argument. "But isn't it the purpose of the gods to be generous?"

"No, dear sister. Generosity is for mortals."

Ilmatar grew frustrated with Ukko's opinion. "Well, if they pray for a loaf of bread, I'm giving them two loaves of bread."

"Your obsession with this planet is unhealthy. Your place is up here with me, like it's always been. It's not even your planet, it's mine."

Ilmatar was shocked. "There's nothing wrong with bringing new life to new worlds, is there? What's wrong with spending time on one of those planets?"

"Your place is here with me, not held down by some foolish planet.

You can never return from the planet if you go down there, you know. The gravity will keep you there forever because you're a giant. I won't be able to bring you back."

"And what if I wanted to stay down there among the people of Santara?"

"I would have to make you smaller, or else you would crush these people you care about so much when you land. Sure, you'll get what you want, but you'll still be trapped there. And if you turn back into a giant to escape, you'll crush the same people you claim to care so much about!"

"But, Ukko, I told you, I don't care if I come back. I want to nurture the good people on Santara." Ilmatar turned away from him, looking back at the ocean, captivated by the harp music.

"Don't you turn your back on me, Ilmatar," Ukko screamed. "Your place is up here, not down there. Who will take care of your part of the nebula if you leave?"

"You take care of it, brother! You seem to have plenty of energy!"

Ukko sent a bolt of lightning flaring past her, but she ignored his threats, since he was so fond of making them.

Ilmatar kept staring at the bright blue oceans of Santara, tears forming in the corners of her eyes. "But Ukko, dear brother, we are gods. Our purpose is to enrich the universe! I could do so much more good if I was down there closer to them."

Ukko had been twisting and steaming through the heavens, but he could take no more. He lunged at her with all his might, and Ilmatar turned to witness the source of the terrific noise Ukko was making.

Roaring in anger, he raged at his innocent sister as the nebula crackled with aggression. Lightning spurted between the columns of gas around them, and Ilmatar backed away from him, terrified of his fury.

"You want to be down there so bad? It's already dragging you down!"

Gravity pulled her down.

"Fine! Be down there!"

Ukko shot another huge bolt at her from the lightning rod, shocking and unbalancing her, forcing her deeper into the gravity well.

Ilmatar began falling to Santara. At first, the feeling was scary, but as she continued falling, she smiled up at her brother, remembering that he had given her what she wanted against his will—her freedom.

The falling became a greeting, a welcoming, and she turned to face the breathtaking blue of the ocean below her as it rushed up to greet her.

Falling closer and closer, she saw continents, ice caps, and volcanoes, and everything else Santara had to offer in intricate detail. She was astonished, to see how complex and amazing the new world she had chosen to call home really was. The closer she got, the louder the harp music became, and as she fell, she fancied that a symphony was greeting her arrival with an orchestra of harps. Then she heard voices singing, "Ilmatar, sweet Ilmatar, Goddess of the Northern Sky!" and she realized they were serenading her.

Ilmatar was thrilled that the people of Santara were singing her praises, and vowed to thank them one day for their beautiful music. Then the waves grew larger beneath her, and she crashed into the deep waters. The wave dissipated long before it reached the shore. The people by the ocean noticed some high swells cresting far from shore, and that was all.

As the water accepted her, she began to float, long before she reached the seafloor. Ukko's lightning no longer troubled Ilmatar. Her new world was extremely peaceful, a deep ocean that could absorb the strongest storm.

Ilmatar felt free for the first time ever, free from the chaos of the nebula and free from her violent brother. The oceans were warm and quiet. Deep inside these waters, she floated, peaceful, calm, and serene, like the ocean surrounding her.

The music passed away from her hearing, and sounds of war and fighting replaced it. She could bear the screams of dying men no longer, and after some time, her head rose above the surface.

She looked in the distance and saw an evil king trying to take over a peaceful kingdom. Weary of the murder and pillage, Ilmatar surged out of the ocean and sent a wave of water rushing across the battlefield that sucked the mad king far out to sea, where he met an agonizing end by drowning.

Chapter Two

Many years later, when the sound of music on harps, flutes, drums, and other new instruments had returned to her ears, Ilmatar rose above the water. She looked all around, taking in the wondrous beauty of the islands on the horizon, and gave thanks to the god of her ocean, Ahto.

Her shimmering blue body had now filled with water, and was translucent and vibrant in the sun. Her hair had become green like the seaweed after so long in the ocean. The ocean had accepted her, and she had become as one with it.

Now it was time for her to create a new god, one born of a marriage between sea and sky. In her long centuries swimming, Ilmatar had listened carefully as the ocean slowly revealed its plan to her in the quiet whispers of the deep, calm sea. Now she knew it was time to do what she wanted to do all those years ago and bring new life to Santara through the birth of a new god. Secure in her ocean domain, she gradually lifted one giant leg to the surface.

Far away, the leg slowly rose. Her knee became a massive plateau between the slopes of her legs, dozens of feet wide, rising high and secure feet above the waves that crashed along her thighs. By the time her legs were positioned, daylight had come and the day was quite warm. Years and years of living in the cold ocean water had thickened the lava that powered her massive body and cooled it to solid rock.

Night was upon the ocean when she arose, and the first things she witnessed were the two yellow moons, shining down on the water in the darkness of night like beacons, lighting her way to safety. She traveled slowly to the place where she felt the most secure, and began to prepare for the new goddess.

As the solid rock of her legs absorbed the heat of the local star, the thick warm lava began to melt deep inside her and flow again, heating her knee from within. New gods and goddesses were only created in warm places, because a great deal of heat and energy was needed to create them. The ocean made her feel secure and kept her flowing lava cool.

A giant seagull spotted the plateau and quickly homed in on the flat area, landing and shaking its wings to straighten its feathers. Then the seagull looked up at Ilmatar, and she knew it was a messenger from the god that ruled her ocean. The seagull spoke with its mind, for her head was quite far away.

Ilmatar learned that this seagull was here to help her bring a new goddess to Santara, one capable of ruling the ocean or the sky with equal power and strength no matter its domain. The God of the Sea and Seagulls would be very proud of her. She learned that the name of this goddess would be told to her in time.

She smiled deeply because she knew her instinct to bring a new god into the world was a premonition of this moment, and thanked the seagull for its divine blessing.

The seagull carefully built a nest, bringing back driftwood in her massive beak. Then it laid three eggs inside the nest, each one bigger than the harvested driftwood. The seagull sat down on the broad eggs to protect them.

Ilmatar was so far away from the landmass on the horizon the highest hills were only specks in the distance. She smiled and rested in the warm water; she was happy with the new creation she had helped with. She was sure that nothing could harm her new eggs this far out at sea. Besides, very little trouble had occurred on Santara since she had drowned the evil king.

Ilmatar was extremely grateful for this blessing. For air married with sea, and giving birth to air again would create powerful offspring, a creature with such great command of the elements that even her brother Ukko would respect her creation, and hopefully begin to respect her, as well.

She would raise her new god to be generous and peaceful and protective of this magical planet, not violent and vindictive like Ukko.

Just when Ilmatar was beginning to relax her guard, fireballs began to tear through the atmosphere of Santara, leaving dark clouds in their wake that billowed and expanded behind them, pouring hot rain across the ocean. Destructive winds shrieked and threatened the plateau. The seagull hunched over the eggs and protected them as well as she could.

Ilmatar thought it was her brother Ukko trying to intimidate her into abandoning her mission, but she was not so easily swayed. As the storms began, Ilmatar raised her hand to serve as a shield to protect the seagull and the sacred eggs from the worst of the storm's fury.

She could hear the farmers praying to Ukko for relief from the storm, and she wondered if he would listen to them, as he had promised her long ago that he would always listen to the prayers of the people.

Much to Ilmatar's surprise, the prayers worked, and a huge wind blew in from the North, blowing the firestorm away from the land to where it landed harmlessly in the ocean.

Ilmatar had been confident in the stability of the great plateau, but during the storm, the fragile elements composing the goddess had been shaken up by the force of the waves crashing on the slopes of her legs.

The fireballs warming the ocean gradually damaged her body until she felt uncomfortably hot instead of warm and she realized the balance of nature was becoming upset.

The lava heating the plateau, agitated by the storms, began to simmer and boil within her to such an extent that she could no longer control the pressure inside. As lava began to pour out of her knee, rolling across the plateau towards the eagle's nest, the eagle screamed and flew away in panic, abandoning the eggs to save herself.

The lava surrounded the driftwood, and at first smoke, then flames, lifted into the air. She cried out in fear as she hemorrhaged, realizing the danger the eggs were in.

Ilmatar knew her only hope was to extinguish the fire in the sea, protecting the eggs with her powers. She summoned all her divine power and cast a protective ward around the eggs. Then she lowered her massive leg into the ocean so the cold water would cool the eggs and preserve them.

Huge waves thundered in all directions, cresting and breaking from their excessive height and rolling away toward the land. These waves were broken up by the powerful winds of the storm pressing against her.

As her leg descended, bubbles of lava struck the water, sending plumes of steam hissing into the air. The eggs descended, protected by the nest, the thick bed of trees burning from the bottom up, heating the eggs slowly, but still protecting them with the branches that had yet to catch fire.

Ilmatar hoped she had enough time as her leg continued to descend, but her large body took significant time to move at all in the gravity of this planet, time she could not afford as the flames licked ever higher, threatening the eggs with a fiery demise. As her leg descended, she lowered her head as well, so that she could observe the eggs when they landed in the water.

The flaming nest struck the water and broke apart, sending the eggs flying into the air momentarily before spinning back to the sea.

The shock of the turbulent seawater on the hot eggs was more force than her protection ward could absorb. Before her eyes, the sacred eggs shattered into thousands of pieces and disappeared into the ocean as her green eyes sunk beneath the water, hot tears mixing with the seawater and warming her cheeks as she slowly submerged.

The protection ward she had cast was stronger than she thought, for when she looked underwater, she saw the shards of the eggs floating down gently, lines of bubbles floating to the surface. It was a magical sight, but meaningless if the eggs were destroyed.

The protection ward began to sparkle even brighter, collecting magic from the power-filled ocean and increasing.

Ilmatar continued to gaze in amazement as her ward began to pull the many shards of the eggs together into one big egg, more powerful than the ones before it. The surface was all different colors, a majestic patchwork of shards, and the newly formed egg was almost as big as the nest that had carried it. Ilmatar realized this would become a splendid god.

A deep blue glow surrounded the new egg, pulsating like a heartbeat. It grew faster until the throbbing pulse under the waves became a thunderous pounding, as the intensity of the magic grew stronger.

The deep blue transformed to a bright blue, and finally a spectacular white, before the entire egg burst apart and her new baby was hatched into the ocean.

Ilmatar stared in wonder. This new baby was a mixture of sea and sky, a powerful force even as an infant. Almost like a whale, this great ocean creature was massive even at birth. She had small wings, which

Ilmatar knew would grow longer in time, and a long flowing tail laced with row after row of colors.

Sea women with long flowing tails and lovely green hair surrounded Ilmatar, swimming in circles. "We are the Nakki," said several of them. "We shall protect you."

Ilmatar stared at this god before her, reaching out to hold her baby. As she did so, a name rang clear in her mind, and she who he was beyond a shadow of a doubt.

"Come here, Loviatar!" The young god recognized her name immediately and turned to her mother with wide eyes.

As the young god reached back for her mother, long, twisting billows of thick black ink surrounded the newly hatched baby and dragged her away, leaving her mother to wail in grief for her stolen child. Being so devoted to compassion and nurturing, she couldn't save her child as a goddess. She knew she needed her brother Ukko's help, far up in the nebula, and his name escaped her lips again and again.

The Nakki were also horrified that they couldn't protect the child, even with their own strength. They spoke to each other solemnly, then nodded and turned as a group to face the sky. The Nakki joined her in mourning as well, singing out,

"Here the heart sighs and eyes are filled with tears.

There, the heart is happy and eyes are showing the joy.

On the wings of hope fly over there, my little heart.

Because there is my home land and I want to go there."

The song of the Nakki resonated in harmonies that rose out of the ocean, along with Ilmatar's cries, and as she learned the haunting melody, her voice joined the Nakki in mourning. Their voices soared out of the sky into the nebula, bouncing off each other and becoming stronger as they floated through the plasma, until the sounds finally reached Ukko's ears.

Chapter Three

Ukko was floating around the nebula. It was almost premium harvesting season, but the lightning and balls of energy were already becoming stronger and denser, providing more energy for Ukko to capture in his long nets.

In the distance, Ukko heard the sound of mourning melodies and recognized Ilmatar's voice. He spun around in surprise.

Although Ilmatar had been preoccupied with life on Santara, Ukko knew that over seven hundred years had already passed since she had fallen to the surface, and seven hundred years was a long time to keep something in memory, even for a god.

He had been so busy harvesting that he had forgotten about the planet of Santara, hunting instead through the arms of the nebula where many more planets were still being formed from the interstellar dust. When he heard Ilmatar's song, it all came back to him suddenly, and he pulled in his nets, abandoning the harvest.

Ukko left the distant arm of the nebula, quickly traveling to Santara where it lay in the heart of his domain, hundreds of years erasing the bitterness in his heart.

"What's the matter, Ilmatar?" Ukko looked down from the heavens, shocked to see a goddess, much less his own sister, mourning.

"Someone took my daughter!" Ilmatar wailed.

"What?" Ukko was surprised at the news. "I've been out by Orsako, mining for energy. I've been taking care of your part of the nebula too, so I've been very busy. Please tell me more about what's going on. I haven't seen you in hundreds of years!"

"But your wind came down and blew the fire away. You must have had something to do with that!" Ilmatar was still upset. Tears continued to fall into the sea.

"I told you, I've been out by Orsako." Ukko was getting frustrated. "Tell me more!"

Ilmatar sobbed up at Ukko. "I had just hatched an egg. Then a rain of fire came down from the sky, and a great wind came down and blew the fire into the sea. Then my eggs turned into one big egg, and a new goddess was born, and I named her Loviatar. But then this black ink flowed through the sea and took my baby! What is going on, brother?"

Ukko's eyes flashed with knowledge. "The only time I have seen that power was when fighting a demon from the Land of the Dead, that strange world the people of Santara call Tuonela. You need to be like one of them, a mere mortal, to enter the Land of the Dead. The portal is far too small for someone like us."

"But what about the wind?" asked Ilmatar. "Someone sent out a great wind."

Recognition filled Ukko's eyes. "That would be Kave, our cousin. You know how he likes to intervene. Have you been living down here so long you've forgotten Kave?"

Ilmatar relaxed at the explanation, knowing that Kave was one of the most benevolent of the Sky Gods. But soon another detail occurred to her that brought her to despair again. "But Kave's intervention only helped the people of Santara, dear brother! They prayed to you for mercy, but he helped instead. The fireballs heated the water until I overheated, destroying the eggs. She came into the world too soon and she couldn't protect herself."

Ukko spoke up immediately, seizing the opportunity to prove his point to Ilmatar. "I have always tried to tell you about the people of Santara, little sister. They only pray for themselves. They don't care what happens to us. The people of Santara are dangerous. Sometimes they get drunk and fight, and other times there are all-out battles. Ilmatar, the only way to get through that portal to the Land of the Dead and get this new goddess to safety is if I turn you into a mortal. But I fear for your safety, too. I fear that you won't like what the people of Santara have become."

"Don't lead me on, Ukko! I'm trying to find my baby. If you can help me, help me, but don't give me false hope."

Ukko smiled. "Oh, dear sister, I forgave you hundreds of years ago. I just want you to be safe. You'll be much smaller, and much more vulnerable. What's even worse, as a mortal, you can actually die. If I lost you forever, I don't know what I would do. To lose one of the gods or goddesses would make the entire nebula unstable. This great heaven relies on us to tend to it. If you died, some of the nebula might even collapse."

"Will you stop worrying about me, Ukko? I can take care of myself! Just turn me into a mortal already so I can start trying to find my way to the Land of the Dead! I can't lose her!"

"Well, prepare then, for your transformation is seconds away. To reach their size is exceedingly painful. I don't want to do this to you, but you insist on finding your daughter. I hope you can forgive me."

"I am willing to do whatever I have to do to find my daughter! Do it!"

Swinging his lightning rod, Ukko cast strong magic down, pulses of light descending to the ocean one after another. As they fell to Santara, pulses of magic covered Ilmatar's gigantic body.

As her body began to shrink, she screamed in intense agony. But the smaller she got, the quieter the screams became because her lungs were shrinking as well. As the spell worked its magic, she began to find the strength to cope with the agony and quietly sink beneath the water, completing her transformation under the sea until the pain stopped.

Ilmatar thought her transformation was completed; she confidently arose from the sea near the coastline. The water splashed away from her as she crested the surface. She was completely nude; perfect blue skin was replaced by a thicker skin the color of sea foam, pale and reflective from the sheen of water across it. Her eyes were small, but deep blue like the ocean, and ferocious and brave. In spite of fitting into the smaller frame of a native of Santara, she had lost none of her charm. Her golden hair shimmered as it cascaded over her shoulders.

With a shock from the cold, Ilmatar fell into the ocean water. She could not breathe underwater anymore, although she had once enjoyed a beautiful union with the sea as a goddess. In her ignorance, she choked on seawater and began to panic, kicking her legs in fear. The strength of her kicks brought her to the surface, and her first memory as a mortal was gorging mouthfuls of seawater, trying to keep her feet moving as she fought for air.

Ilmatar sank beneath the water again, sucking in one last mad breath before going under. She felt her oxygen begin to deplete, and realized she was drowning.

Ilmatar was used to the mind of a goddess, not the raw emotions of people. The terror became a physical threat, clawing at tickling at her lungs like a wild beast, sending snaps and prickles of pain shooting through her arms and legs, sucking at her mouth and begging her to expel the air and give in to the water. Everything grew darker until Ilmatar could see no more.

But in her blindness, four of the Nakki lifted her up on their backs and brought Ilmatar to the surface. She floated, half-awake and wrapped in the Nakki's six arms that reminded her of butterfly legs, like a protective cocoon. Another Nakki floated before her and kept her head elevated. The other two pounded her back with their arms to force the fluid from her drowning lungs. The pressure on her back released the pressure in her lungs, and she snapped her eyes wide open.

She coughed violently, releasing the water. She began to realize she must have inhaled more water, as everything was going black.

The Nakki kept a firm and protective hold on Ilmatar the whole time, keeping her above the surf as she caught her breath. Only once she had recovered did the Nakki move closer to the shore.

Because they were sea creatures, the Nakki dropped her legs once she could reach the bottom, and Ilmatar stood up in the surf by the shore.

Once Ilmatar caught her breath and could stand on her own, the Nakki swam away, for they knew Ilmatar would now have to be on land. If she remained in the water, she would surely drown, for as a goddess, she had never needed to learn how to swim.

She maintained her footing, even though the sand scraped against her new feet quite painfully, and maneuvered her exhausted body through the surf.

The next pounding wave plunged her to the shallow water at the shore where she could reach the bottom with her arms and crawl out to the land that was now home.

Naked, she gasped for air and tried to brush the cold water from her strange new skin. Her body scraped against the sand as she pulled herself further from the sea. She tried to get to her knees, but the weight of her body was painful. She shivered and breathed fast, trying to stay warm as the heat left her body in the cold afternoon air.

Ilmatar pulled herself away from the sand and into the grasses at the edge of the shore. Moving through the grass was easier, but the blades still scraped her legs. Goddesses were not used to bleeding. She touched the strange liquid oozing from her leg and instinctively pushed some herbal leaves upon the cut, not even realizing what she was doing. The pain began to recede.

She reached a bright red barn and hut tucked away into the grass with trees outside. Thin branches had been whittled smooth and stuck between the forks of the trees, allowing whoever lived inside to hang clothes to dry as well as let in the damp seaside air, for the day was still sunny.

She found many clothes, but a long, plain white dress with a red smock sewed above it was the only thing that would fit her. She pulled the dress over her head and headed to the barn to hide. The horses inside were beautiful and covered in chocolate brown hair, but the second they saw her, they began to raise an alarm, stomping their hooves and whinnying loudly.

"Ssh," whispered Ilmatar, trying to calm them.

The horses stared right back at her and stomped their feet defiantly.

"I won't hurt you," she whispered.

The horses would not be so easily calmed. They continued to pound their hooves and cry out in fear. She saw the door of the hut open suddenly, and never having seen the people of Santara before, only hearing awful stories from Ukko, she hid in the second story of the barn, covering herself in hay and trying to stay silent.

Chapter Four

Tuonela was a deep cavern, with a black river slowly flowing through the bottom. Inside was where every soul went when someone died on Santara. They would come here, to this dark land, expecting to find the rulers, Milla and Andri. Instead, they found a ruined world, overrun with flying creatures and twisted demons like Tursas, the evil wizard who had stolen the baby Loviatar. In this land, they would suffer until Tursas absorbed their souls, using their power to fuel his aging and withered heart. Without their power, he would have long since withered into the blood-covered stones.

Tursas had a problem—nobody had been dying. Santara had been enjoying a long period of peace, and Tursas's power was waning quickly.

Lava bubbled from cracks in the earth. Trees long since withered, blackened branches brushing the ground in agony. This was the world of the dead, and many spirits remained here in the river cavern, while many more lay scattered across the desert that stretched out when the river ceased flowing, all the way to the horizon.

The forgotten creatures rested here now, in the forgotten sands. The dragon wings stretched high above the sand beside the unicorn horns, so high the dead traveled beneath them with ease, slowing down, grateful for the shade.

As the Surmas, helpless servants of Tursas, flew through the cavern, their twisted master walked far beneath them, protecting an infant in his arms. That he had stolen the infant was of no consequence to him.

Deep inside the burning realms, where the rocks of time hung miles above, the evil Tursas walked in the deep, among rocks soaked in blood. He walked past a cage in which he had imprisoned Milla, the rightful master of Tuonela, against his mighty will thousands of years ago.

He still survived within the cage, withered and ancient.

Beside him sat his wife, Andri, in another cage, her arm so shriveled from age that she could barely stretch it out towards her husband in the other cage. Never able to touch him, and yet so close, she survived in endless torment.

Andri silently exhaled, her voice long faded and turned to dust. How she longed for her dear husband's touch, though her lips were too old to speak, or even move to take in nutrients anymore. Slowly, ever so slowly, she was starving, and that was the torture—Tursas always fed her just enough to keep surviving.

She knew that Tursas took pleasure in her torment.

The Surmas shrieked and plummeted through the air of the cavern high above, awaiting a promised destiny of peace in the world beyond, but currently trapped to do his bidding until he was done with them.

Unfortunately for the Surmas, Tursas never planned to let them go, but only delivered such promises to keep the flying beasts working for him. Watching them trapped here, between the living and the final resting, excited him too much.

Tursas presented the baby to Milla and Andri, smiling. The young water goddess with wings of the sky smiled peacefully, as Tursas had already put her under a spell. Even a very young goddess could be quite dangerous to a dark wizard, so Tursas had already pacified the newborn creation with dark magic, suppressing her mind.

"I'm going to sacrifice this Goddess Loviatar for my own power, and there's nothing you can do about it!"

Milla stepped forward, grunting in pain. Every step was difficult, and he chose his steps in the tiny cage wisely. Milla had grown so old that even lifting his hand to his mouth to eat what meager food Tursas doled out was becoming a symphony of cracks and pops as his ancient joints fought to remain still and undisturbed. Even though Andri could no longer speak, her husband still had the strength to form words, though he hated his ancient body for rebelling and moving so slowly.

"Please, Tursas, do whatever you want with us, but don't hurt Loviatar! If you do anything to that goddess, you will have every god and goddess trying to find you! They will even search Tuonela. Beware,

Tursas!"

"Too late, Milla. It looks like the balance of power is shifting. That won't be good for the gods, but it will be good for me," said Tursas. "It's time. I must be going." Tursas turned away and descended the long staircase to his haven deep inside Tuonela.

Ancient stone steps led further into the cavern, carved into the wall long ago. Tursas descended until the darkness surrounded him. The baby lay clasped between his hands, his great prize, held like a trophy before him.

Tursas had reached his own stronghold. Deep inside the land of the dead, this cruel wizard had an unusual fate in mind for the small baby in his hands.

He looked down at the creation of the gods, proud of the prize he had grabbed. Unlike normal babies, this was one special child, born of powerful elements and full of rich, magical power. Tursas could use this power to resurrect a dragon from the realm of death. Her blue eyes were like the ocean she had been stolen from. They stared into the dark chambers of the wizard's face.

The darkness of Tuonela had long since taken over the corrupted wizard. As he approached his beloved dragon altar, his face reflected nothing but darkness, for the wizard had long since given his mind back to its maker and retreated into the lands where the disturbed spirits continue to roam.

What lay beyond those endless, shifting sands beyond the black river, in that deep void, no one, not even the evil Tursas, could say. Not even his magic was strong enough to pierce that eternal darkness.

The dragon altar was the standing remains of a dragon leg. The rest of the dragon had been entombed for centuries beneath the strange rocks of the caverns. The massive claw stood upright, balancing a deep basin of water as a permanent sacrifice to Tursas. Now its mighty power served only the dark wizard. Tursas reflected that he would need a new place to put the sacrificial font once the dragon returned to life and ceased to be a motionless instrument.

The wizard placed the baby inside the font on the altar. As he sprinkled dark water across the baby's brow, making her blue eyes blink in confusion, the wizard spoke slowly, condemning her to his curse.

"I curse you to be bonded with the black dragon forever! For all your days, you and the black dragon shall serve only me!"

A huge earthquake began to rattle the cavern, centering on the altar. Tursas fell to the floor, forced to catch himself with his ancient arms.

Tursas rose to a standing position and faced the dragon, which still lay upside down, half-buried in the rocks.

"Nobody can break your curse unless they pierce deep inside the dragon's heart, and only then can you be free. But that's never happened before, so don't get too excited about it! No one has ever survived my curse! I am the Lord of the Dead!" Tursas laughed with pride, and the deep insanity echoed off the walls. "Now I command you to rise, great black dragon. You have been in the rocks for long enough. Rise, and become what you once were, the creature who was never named, for no one who has stepped in his way survived."

The whole cave began to rattle and shake. The deep red clay of the caverns began to shatter and fall away, scattering down the dark slopes. A shriek of pain echoed inside a hidden chamber as the dragon broke free of the ancient stones, powdering the ancient volcanic rock into dust with his might. Tursas knew from this show of force that the baby had been very powerful indeed. The dragon had been given new life, and now what had died long ago was once again reborn.

Tursas was thrilled. A goddess this powerful would surely bring might to the black dragon, the ability to kill the people of Santara so he could wield his power again.

The dragon rose high into the air, turning around to blow hot fire at the wizard. Tursas was unaffected, sweeping his powers in protection around him.

The dragon roared repeatedly in frustration, echoing through the caverns and bringing small rocks crashing down from the ceiling. Thousands of years in the endless realms of Death had left the dragon addled and confused.

The dragon tried to make sense of the ancient creature before him, as Tursas had been a young wizard with a twisted sneer when the dragon had been put to death. Now he shrouded his face in twisting darkness, revealing his snarling wreckage only when he felt safe.

The dragon screamed in confusion, flapping its wings violently, for dragons are very impatient creatures.

"Easy, now, easy. You're wasting your energy. I have a mission for you at daybreak."

The dragon ceased its roaring and landed on a rock, craning forward to listen to Tursas's commands, not realizing how effortlessly the wizard had overruled his mind.

As the quake caused by the dragon's resurrection passed through the cavern, the cages began to shake from side to side, and when the shaking stopped, Andri discovered that for the first time in centuries, the cages were close enough together that she could reach through and touch Milla's hand.

She reached as far as she could between the cages and his hand reached out to meet hers. As they held hands together in the dimness, they smiled at each other. Even though she could speak no words to express her joy at being able to touch her own true soul mate again.

Chapter Five

King Cato walked deep into the Forbidden Forest to reach Lena's house. Lena was one of the last of the Lion People to keep living there. Those who had been completely lions could never return to humanity, for none of their humanity was left.

Most of the people who had been freed from the curse had left the same day the curse was lifted. Over the next few months, the rest of them left as well, leaving only Lena stubbornly determined to live the life of a Lion Person, even though every trace of the lion had been removed from her the second the curse was lifted.

Leko walked alongside Cato, smiling from ear to ear. The walk through the forest was far more pleasant than another day at the castle. Instead of bustling maids, he enjoyed the wild flowers and croaking frogs and whistling birds of the forest.

"Look, Papa!" Leko pointed to some red berries growing on the forest floor.

"Those are lingonberries, my son. They are Lena's favorite. What a great find! We'll be eating pie today for sure! Help me gather some."

Leko was happy to kneel by the bushes. He helped his father gather many berries, and Cato noticed that Leko had gathered even more than he had when they were done. Cato smiled at his son and patted him on the head. "That will make your grandmother very proud, Leko. Let's keep moving."

When they finally reached the clearing, Leko looked at the small cottage where Lena lived. "It looks like the house is part of the forest!" he exclaimed.

The house had indeed been built from many parts of the forest. The windows were wide open, giving plenty of fresh air, and graced with freshly picked boughs. Green plants grew happily on the roof, sustaining the house and creating an enchanting aroma with their small colorful flowers. Vines traveled up and down the edges of the tree, which had been hollowed out years ago to create her home.

"That's the way I used to live too, inside this small dwelling in the forest," answered Cato. "We were at one with the forest, and it became our protector while we were cursed to turn into lions every night. But now we have been freed from the curse, and can live where we please. Let's go inside." Cato knocked on the front door, which had been seamlessly wrought from the tree, surrounded by ivy to make it indistinguishable.

Lena opened the door, white hair flowing from her head.

"Cato! Come in! I haven't seen you in months."

"It's good to see you too, Mother." Cato stepped inside.

Lena beamed with joy when she saw the young child. "Oh, he's so handsome! I've been living out here, and nobody tells me anything anymore. All my friends have left!"

Cato sighed with frustration. "Mother, you know I broke the curse eight years ago. Once it was lifted, all the other people chose a life in the villages outside of the forest. You're the only one still staying here."

Lena glared at Cato stubbornly, stomping her foot in defiance. "Cato! You know how I am! I've lived here my entire life. This is what I know. You can't ask me to change all that! I don't turn into a lion anymore, you made sure of that, but my spirit is still wild. When I sleep at night, the animals in the forest are my symphony. Just let me be in peace."

Cato looked around. The wooden sculptures he had carved as a child sat around the humble cottage, but years of weather had left them moisture-logged and cracked, some broken entirely. "Well, Mother, I've never been able to change your mind, have I? But if you ever do decide to join us at the castle, we'd welcome you with open arms. We have so many empty rooms that we've told the servants to stop dusting some of them because it takes too long. Hey, that reminds me. Leko! Show Lena what you got for her."

Leko brought out the large pile of lingonberries.

Lena looked at them with joy and surprise. "Thank you so much, Leko. How did you know those were my favorite? Cato told you, didn't he?" she asked.

Leko nodded immediately.

"Little grandson, I think you'll find there are many reasons to live in the forest among the animals, and one of them is my lingonberry pies. You two have picked enough for at least three pies. I'd better start mixing these up."

Before long, Lena had made the crumbly crusts and had started loading the berries into them. She wrapped them and placed them over the fire to start cooking. Before long the whole cottage was full of sweet-smelling aromas mixed with the smell of the flowers.

"That smells incredible!" Cato heard a voice outside. "Someone's cooking lingonberries."

Lena stuck her head out the window. "Get in here, Malkin. There's enough pie for everyone!"

Cato immediately rose with politeness when the lion-man entered the room. He was covered from head to toe in thick fur, and many teeth in a powerful jaw smiled at him. Both men gave each other an embrace of long friendship.

"Malkin! How nice to see you again!"

"You as well. I've been on my way to the Land of the Musaat. I seek more inspiration for my tribe."

Cato studied Malkin's lion features. "I'm sorry that I couldn't lift the curse from your people."

Malkin held up his hand in protest. "Say no more. I didn't come here to make you feel bad. Look how many people you saved. Now my son is free to travel as he wishes. If it weren't for you, we'd still be trapped in the forest as well. Now the villagers welcome us, and the fear has faced away."

"How about the other lions? Are they still doing their scouting runs?"

"Every day they go through all of Santara, making sure your kingdom remains safe. Just because it's a time of peace doesn't mean we're going to shirk our duties."

After a great deal of pie, Cato got up from the table, and Leko followed him back home to the castle. The walk home didn't take very long, but Leko had eaten his fill of pie, so the walk seemed to take forever.

Alzena was waiting in the castle and noticed Cato's heavy frown when he took off his crown.

"I can see that visit didn't go very well," said Queen Alzena.

Cato slumped onto the couch while Leko excused himself to go take a nap.

"You know my mother," Cato told the gilded ceiling. "She's very set in her ways."

"Someday, when you least expect it, Cato, she'll come around. Every woman changes her mind from time to time, and when she does, it's her business, not yours. That's just the way we are."

Cato kept looking at the ceiling, but felt more at ease.

Chapter Six

The great black dragon flew across the open ocean, flying for the coastline of Santara. Deep inside the black dragon, the young goddess struggled ferociously. She had been reduced to a construct of the dragon, surviving only to feed energy to it, to keep it alive. Loviatar loathed her captivity, and wished that the evil creature had remained dead, buried in the rock, for then she would not be here, trapped inside.

Loviatar struggled hard enough to break free of her prison inside the heart of the dragon. She pushed toward the dragon's massive head, fleeing its twisted, withered heart, willing her consciousness forward.

Loviatar detested being separated from her physical form. Her enslavement to the dragon had stripped her of her physical presence and left behind a pure version of her, one that could move freely to the black dragon's mind now.

She could tell that the dragon had been weakened by her escape, but it was by no means defeated. It swept through the air, relentlessly closing in on the shores of Santara. Although she had managed to slow its progress, she had not stopped the dragon's flight. She knew she had to take more desperate measures if she wanted to escape, and decided to start attacking its mind, which floated before her in the strange spiritual world Tursas's curse had sentenced her to exist in.

Loviatar used her significant mental presence to pound on the black dragon's mind, relentlessly flailing at its defenses with her powerful wings. Even as a spirit, she had the same qualities as the living goddess. When that had no effect, she pounded her astral body against his mind in frustration, trying to break through his defenses.

She was close enough to sense the black dragon's thoughts. Vivid images from the dragon's subconscious revealed to her how he planned to capture souls to feed the mad Tursas.

Loviatar had seen enough. She rebelled with everything she had, pounding against the dragon's mind. "Stop!" she screamed. "You have to stop!" As she realized the consequences of being stuck inside this dragon as he committed ungodly acts, she screamed again. "You can't do this! You'll upset the very balance of nature! You have to stop! Stop! Are you listening to me?"

The dragon became aware of the irritating presence of Loviatar. Her aggression only served to irritate, and waves of rage powered along the smooth pathways of the black dragon's mind. The hate swept over Loviatar, lifting her off the surface of his mind and thrusting her back into the deep oblivion of his tortured heart, where she had been trapped before.

As the ropes of hatred pulled her down into the depths of the black dragon and tied her there, trapping her in horror, Loviatar quietly began to lose her sanity and everything started to fade away.

The dragon rejoiced at the forced submission of the irritating creature he was unwillingly tethered to. He spewed hot waves of fire before him, although they were sucked into the wide reaches of the ocean below and quickly extinguished in clouds of steam.

The dragon saw a village on the coastline and approached with astonishing speed, speed that he had recovered once he forced the goddess to submit. The farmers ran for cover while the dragon flew across the beach and toward the village. They ducked; he billowed fire from his belly. Lions standing on their hind legs ran out of the forest, throwing heavy rocks at the black dragon. Although they fell short of hitting him, it enraged him, and he began to flex his tail, impatient for the slaughter to begin.

The villagers were all terrified by his massive talons and the huge spikes on his tail. As he flew over, he picked one of the young women up with his long tail. The spikes wrapped around her, impaling her, and her screams turned to gurgling as she passed away. The dragon unhooked his tail and shook her loose, letting her fall to the rooftops below. Her soul rose, as did every soul that followed in her path, claimed by the dragon so he could feed it to Tursas.

The dragon opened its mouth again, and the spikes on his face began to glow red from the heat. He poured the fire across the barn, scorching it hot enough to set the straw within burning yellow in seconds.

The villagers screamed even louder, pouring out of their hiding places and trying to put out the fire as the dragon flew inland. As it passed, it also set the mill ablaze, and people started to try to put the other fire cut, as well.

The dragon thought all was well, but soon he was being pummeled with big rocks. He was not pleased with this, and blew fire at them. He was even more annoyed when they avoided the fire and continued to hurl rocks.

The dragon thought this a mere nuisance until one of the rocks tore through his wing, leaving a small hole. He could still fly, but not nearly as fast. As he lost altitude, he decided to really scare the lions, so he swooped down as low as he could over their heads before continuing his path of destruction.

The lions were unperturbed by this display, and continued to hurl rocks as he circled.

One messenger escaped on horseback and fled for the castle of Santara. The other refugee was not so lucky and was yanked from his horse by the massive tail of the dragon, leaving the one man alive to bring the critical message to King Cato. The dragon traveled deeper towards the castle, south to attack another village first, down by the dark forest that separated the land. He could not see through the trees, no matter how hard he scanned as he flew over, finding his vision blocked by thick green leaves at every turn, providing him no view of the forest floor.

As he returned to attack the village, more lions emerged from the fields and he was surprised he hadn't seen them hiding. This time, the rocks were even heavier, and one struck his tail with enough force to break his hardened scales, sending the large black disks clattering to the ground below. The dragon turned away from the village and glided quite slowly toward the castle in the distance.

As he flew off towards Santara, the lions gathered together to discuss their plans. Their leader, Malkin, was larger than the rest, and immediately laid out the plan.

"Let's use the passageways in the forest. This dragon has never been here before. He has no idea about the secret tunnels. We should hurry, while it's distracted. The rest of you should stay here and put the fires out."

The other lions nodded and ran for the Forbidden Forest as quickly as possible. The rest ran back to the village by the shore to help the survivors.

When they got back to the village, the barn was still burning, but the villagers had managed to extinguish the mill. The Lion-People ran back and forth from the ocean, carrying large buckets of water to dump on the fire. Because they were far stronger than the villagers, they could carry more water, and before long, the barn had been put out as well.

Malkin knew the way through the secret passages very well. Long before the dragon had reached the castle, Malkin had already reached the library, closing the secret door behind him by pushing the handle. The door slowly returned to being a section of the wall. He jumped up the spiral stairs two or three at a time while the door was still closing and made his way to the throne room.

When Malkin entered, one of the advisors pointed in alarm. "What's this creature doing here?"

Cato turned around.

"Him? That's Malkin! He's one of the best warriors in the kingdom. He's saved many of your villages from danger. Show him some respect. If he's here, something terrible must be happening."

The advisor bowed his head. "You are right, as always, my king."

"What's the matter, Malkin?" Cato asked.

"We're under attack by a fearsome black dragon right now!"

King Cato immediately rose from his throne. "Ready my armor!" he commanded.

"Father, I'm scared!" Leko stood by his side, but his legs shook and he looked sweaty and pale.

Cato took his young son's hand and held it in his own, gripping it tightly. "It is time to be brave, son. You need to go somewhere safe."

Leko returned the grip, holding on so hard Cato feared he would never let go. "Where do I go?"

"The safest place for you is the library. Go there now. Passages exist from the library to the sanctuary, in case the palace was ever attacked. The Chamber of the Tomes is next to a round stone on the wall where you press in the middle. This will open a passage leading you to the sanctuary. In the sanctuary, you will find Silve the knight. Go to him now. He will help you escape."

Leko ran off down the hallway, and when he was out of sight and safe, Cato breathed a sigh of relief and turned, ready for battle.

Chapter Seven

Leko ran down the hallway, and not too far from the throne room, he spied the spiral staircase that led to the library. He went down the twisting staircase quickly, but not too quickly, because he knew it would make his head spin and he would fall. A huge roar from the dragon echoed even underground.

As soon as he reached the library, he saw his mother and Margaret at the other end.

Alzena pressed a round stone in the wall, and the doorway began to slowly open. "Hurry!" she cried. "Dragons don't waste any time!"

Leko ran for the back of the library.

"I hope this is the last time in my life I ever have to use this escape route!" Margaret huffed as Leko ran over.

As Leko got closer, he saw that Alzena was holding his baby sister, Nova, and began to relax. The doorway was too narrow to escape through yet, and he had to wait with the rest of them as the door ground on ancient gears deep below the floor.

"How did you know about that door?" Leko asked.

"When I was six years old, the Bowmen were wild riders of the north, and my father was warring with them. They attacked the castle, and I had to use this same door to escape back then. Now it's wide enough. Hurry!"

Margaret hurried into the corridor and Leko followed close behind, Queen Alzena bringing up the last of them and holding the baby safe in one arm, quite tight; she used her other arm to press the other stone to shut the door behind them.

Once she heard the gears starting to roll and moan again, she turned and hurried down the corridor to catch up with Leko and Margaret.

The corridor nestled underneath the castle, in the deep dungeons, was marked with red stones so they wouldn't lose their way in the maze. A series of airways provided fresh air and circulation underground. It also kept the castle quite cool during the summer.

Alzena hurried through the corridor; she heard a loud roaring far above her. She knew a dragon roar when she heard one, and she began to breathe faster, realizing it was right above her castle. Fire bloomed out of the vent, expanding underneath the castle. She realized the corridor would be in danger. She saw a wide column not far from Leko and Margaret, and screamed, "The column!"

Margaret turned to look and headed for it as quickly as she could. Leko looked around, confused, and Alzena knew she had to act with haste, because the flames were billowing closer. She grabbed Leko with her other arm, swinging him to the side as they both ran as for the thick stone column supporting the castle above.

Queen Alzena dove behind it, just as the fire shot behind her, burning her shoe clean off her foot and singing the dress hard enough to set it on fire.

She screamed in pain. Leko came over to her, grabbing tiny Nova and carrying her to safety while Alzena rolled her burning dress out of the way of the flames.

As the flames died away, a knight dressed in the full battle armor of Santara, glistening silver from head to toe, ran to their aid from the far end of the corridor.

"Sir Silve!" cried Alzena.

The knight grabbed his canteen and poured his water over the flames consuming her dress. The fabric sizzled, but dutifully was extinguished.

"Your Highness! You've been burned! We have to get you all to safety!"

The royal family, the nanny, and Sir Silve all escaped the dangerous passageway to the sanctuary beyond.

The quiet forest was peaceful, and deep inside was Lena's cottage, where Alzena rested. Alzena's baby was in her arms, crying and scared. Leko sat beside his mother in the cot where she rested. Lena took care of the burns on Alzena's foot as they relaxed in the safety of the sanctuary.

Alzena knew she had to calm her children down before they drew any attention to themselves they didn't want. So she began to sing them a lullaby she had heard long ago when she was just a child herself.

"Even though you are playful,
Even though you are sulky,
Even when I spoil you,
You look at me and I see your sweetness."

Over and over again, she sang to her children, rocking Nova where she rested, cradled in the crook of her arm, while her other arm softly stroked Leko's hair, soothing him to sleep as the melody floated up and down. The song lulled the young children into secure sleep while they rested in the quiet forest.

Chapter Eight

A loud commotion broke out behind Cato, with the bang of a door being thrown open and many soldiers talking at once. Cato turned to the door, where his armor had arrived. It shone brilliantly, full of power from the Goddess of Light, and so heavy that only he could wear it. The squires helped him into it, and when Cato had been shielded, he was a brilliant sight to behold.

He put General Eino's cloak over his armor. The massive red velvet garment was still preserved after these hundreds of years since his grandfather had been turned into one of the three original Lion-People. The gold embroidered around the hem was still intact, holding it together with great strength so that, even now, not a stitch was out of place.

Cato exited the castle, entering the courtyard at full speed on his horse. Looking up, he saw that the dragon was flying overhead, huge black wings blocking out the sun.

The dragon breathed hot fire down from his mouth, and it raced across the towers, turning the flags into triangles of flames.

"Quickly! Shut the vents! There are women and children down there!"

Three of the bowmen started turning the large crank. Cato looked around, nervous. It turned slowly, weighted down by all the pulleys and ropes holding down the vent covers. As the vent groaned in protest, the dragon loomed closer, swooping down to get a better shot.

"Hurry!" roared Cato, never taking his eyes off the dragon.

As the creature drew close, he sent another huge wave of fire at the windows. Cato watched in horror as the fireball began to pour into the vents by the castle, sweeping through the underground.

When the dragon came around, he dipped low enough that he would fly right over Cato, who quickly wielded the great Sword of Light, which was the way he preferred his transformative weapon to stay, and managed to get a lucky swipe across his thick belly scales.

Black blood began to pour from the wound and over Cato, entering his armor through the faceplate, which had to be left open for breathing. The hot blood stung his skin with some unknown poison, and he roared in tandem with the dragon. As it dripped away, Cato found he could cope with the pain when his kingdom was in danger.

The dragon possessed great strength, but it also possessed enough intelligence to know remaining here was fruitless. Attacking more helpless villagers was a better option for collecting many souls in a short amount of time, and he flew in that direction.

Cato's bowmen, mounted on horseback, had managed to reach the courtyard by this point, and Cato pointed across the bridge with his sword after the fleeing dragon.

The bowmen took off, and when it was clear for him to cross, Cato stirred his horse to action. The horse was terrified by the massive dragon but ran forward at Cato's command, leaping into action to overcome the fear.

Cato rode at full speed and kept riding until he reached the village where the black dragon had directed his wrath. Cato could see smoke on the horizon from the fires still burning in the villages by the shore, and knew if he didn't stop the dragon, he would burn his whole kingdom to the ground.

The bowmen kept their bowstrings busy, shooting arrow after arrow. The repeated attacks drove the dragon to land on the ground, where he was easier to shoot. The bowmen continued to pepper him with arrows, but other than irritating him, they seemed to serve no purpose. They broke when they hit the strong scales and fell to the ground.

When Cato was a safe distance from the dragon, he dismounted and quickly pulled his weapon. One of the bowmen got too close, and the giant talons of the dragon's claw buried themselves into his chest as the huge leg came crashing down. The bowmen stopped moving instantly, and when the claw lifted into the air again, they stayed still.

The dragon spewed fire this way and that, burning some of the bowmen's arms. They screamed in pain, rolling on the ground to extinguish the flames.

Cato knelt, distant from the main battle, and grateful for the bowmen keeping the mighty dragon busy. One bowman with long brown hair screamed as the dragon picked him up in his jaws and hurled him across the field, where he rolled and lay still for several seconds before lifting his neck.

Cato thought for a few seconds after seeing the fallen bowman.

"Goddess of Light, shine down and help me pierce the dragon's heart!"

As he cast his prayer, another bowman fell from a crushing stomp.

Magically, Cato's weapon transformed into a mighty sword, and Cato raced across the field, full of fury and vengeance. He buried the sword in between the scales of the dragon's belly. The sword sizzled inside the dragon, and the scales fell to the ground, dislodged by the powerful weapon.

The dragon roared in pain and shook violently, wrenching himself free of the sword and leaping into the air. He hovered, blowing fire madly, before turning and flying back towards the ocean, dripping black blood across the rocks.

The soldiers cheered, "Three cheers for King Cato!"

Chapter Nine

Ilmatar huddled under the straw, listening intently to the voices below the floorboards. They used hushed tones and careful phrasing.

"Hush, Penelope," whispered a husky old man. "You'll scare Beanie."

One of the horses, probably Penelope, cried out distrustfully again. A wheedling female voice broke out. "Oh, hush up, Beanpole, I know you always do what the other horses do."

At the female's voice, the horses began to calm. Ilmatar crept out of the straw and stuck her head down the staircase to see two people.

The man and woman were still walking around the stables, petting the horses and soothing them by feeding them apples, which they happily crunched. As soon as the horses spied Ilmatar again, they resumed their banging on the floorboards and knocking their heads against the doors of their stalls.

"Whoa, guys! What's going on?"

"I think you should look behind you," said the woman slowly.

The old man turned around, revealing his bright red vest and thick work shirt tucked beneath, and stared curiously at Ilmatar as she perched atop the stairs, afraid to move a muscle.

"Well, I daresay that dress looks better on her than it ever did on you, Leona!"

"Watch your tongue, Benno! Come down here, lady, we're not going to hurt you."

Ilmatar took one step at a time, but as she descended, her feet chafed against the raw wood steps and the cuts opened up again. She flinched and struggled to maintain her composure as she headed down the long staircase.

"Oh, for the love of the gods, Benno, she's bleeding! What happened to this poor creature? Go help her down the stairs!"

Benno hurried up the stairs and obligingly held out his arms. Ilmatar happily relaxed into his very strong hold and allowed her tired body to be carried down the staircase.

"You be gentle with her now," declared Leona. "Get her into the house where I can take care of her properly. She can't be out here with all the straw and manure."

With a single soft grunt, Benno walked out of the barn and through the field, back to the house, where he set her down on a soft bed and started working on stoking up the fire against the cold outside, all without saying anything else.

Leona entered as well. "That's better," she said. "Now, where did I put that cream?"

She started opening cupboards one by one, and as they fell into silence, the quiet house became interrupted only by the crackling fire and the slamming of cupboards.

Leona set to work finding her other medicines while Benno silently added more wood to the fire. The smell of burning cedars was intoxicating to Ilmatar, and she felt very relaxed. Back in the thick plasmas of the nebula all those centuries ago, the wood-smoke passed clearly to her senses as she hovered over Santara, and had remained a welcoming aroma to her ever since.

Ukko called the roasting meat on the fires "sacrifices." Ilmatar was more content to bless their meals, and sent blessings to the people of Santara, seeing them as gifts rather than sacrifices.

She stared at both Leona and Benno's clothing, examining every detail, having never seen people from Santara before. Even though they were tattered, they were warm clothes. The woman was wearing a green smock and a white apron. The man was wearing thick blue pants, a warm brown shirt, and an even warmer red vest that had clearly been stuffed with feathers.

The cabin was very modest, not like the grand palaces of the gods. Inside the simple hut, she saw only a fireplace, two tables, and one bed, all of them quite humble.

"Do mortals always live this way?" Ilmatar asked aloud.

"Well, not all of them," answered Benno. "The Lion-People lived quietly in the woods for hundreds of years not too far from here. They lived in harmony with the forest until their curse was lifted. But there has always been a king in Santara, one after another, or sometimes queens, and they all live in a big fancy castle way over there past the Forbidden Forest."

"What a horrid name for something as holy as a forest. I hope they find a new name for it soon." The idea of a forest being "forbidden" repulsed Ilmatar, because nothing was truly forbidden to the gods and goddesses.

The old lady brought forward a strong smelling bowl with a wooden spoon inside. She was confused, because gods and goddesses did not eat food like the mortals did. The old lady smiled at her and picked up her own spoon. She put the thick meat and vegetables in her mouth and chewed.

Ilmatar was more than happy to follow her example. The soup was hot and pleasing to her cold stomach, and as she got used to human food, she absorbed the strong taste of the meat and the soft vegetables, learning the new flavors with each spoonful. As she ate the soup, she felt the pain and stiffness leave her mortal body.

"Mojakka," said the woman, pointing to the bowl.

"This is mojakka? This is incredible. No wonder you enjoy life here so much."

The old lady smiled. "What a strange woman! I bid you welcome to Farralina."

"And where are we exactly?"

"In the great kingdom of Santara, in a faraway corner. We survive on the fish and the fruits of the earth."

Ilmatar turned to the aging Benno. "What do you do around here?"

The old man spoke with a deep voice, but Ilmatar sensed no threat from him either. She began to wonder if Ukko had even been telling the truth about the people of Santara. "Me? I've been fishing here my whole life."

Ilmatar gasped at his weathered hands, beaten by the elements for decades. Deep cracks covered them in maps of valleys. She winced in reaction.

Leona glanced down at Ilmatar's feet. "Oh, dear woman, your feet are bleeding badly! I need to start taking care of you right away."

Leona grabbed one of the jars full of paste she had collected and started rubbing it into Ilmatar's injured feet with her bare hands. Instantly, the soft cream started working its way into her bleeding feet, and before long they had been cleansed and no longer stung or tingled.

Ilmatar watched silently as she wrapped her feet in clean cloth, then gave her a good solid pair of walking shoes made of soft bark woven in a basket style that had been baked to harden and strengthen them against the sand.

"I am Ilmatar, dear friends. I am on a long journey. I need to visit Tuonela."

"Heavens, no!" Leona cried. Her face went pale as she stepped forward, wringing her hands. "Why would you want to go to a place like that? No mortal faces death willingly. It makes me wonder if you are even human yourself, if it weren't for your bleeding feet."

"I am human now, but I was once a goddess. You need to help me get to the Land of the Dead as soon as possible. I'm on a very important quest."

"But your feet need as much healing as possible!"

Ilmatar shook her head. "The longer I stay here, the more danger my daughter is in."

Leona sighed deeply, but acknowledged her with a nod. "You're right, of course. There's a tavern half a mile back from the coast, by the lone rock. You can't miss it. It's the biggest rock for miles. You'll find people that can help you there. If there's anybody that knows more about Tuonela or knows how to help you, you will find them there." Leona held forth extra cloth bandages and cream.

Ilmatar stepped forward to accept them. The four steps forward were excruciating, even with the healing paste applied, but she stubbornly pressed forward, accepting the medicine and placing it on the table with other supplies they provided for her, such as cloudberries, small round loaves of bread, and dried meat in a large pouch, which she arranged in a satchel they gave her.

"I can't thank you enough for your help," said Ilmatar. Her feet were still sorer than she would care to admit, but she had a pressing fear within her gut that pushed her forward on her mission.

Leona handed her a walking stick. "You need this, it will help you. It helped my grandfather when he had trouble walking. You may have been a goddess once, but as you said, you are a mortal now, and this walking stick can help you. If I were you, I would tell no one about where you came from, or who you are. There are many people here in Farralina that love to take advantage of people any chance they can get. You need to be careful when you are on your quest."

Accepting the walking stick with gratitude, Ilmatar answered her support with a prayer. "If I was still a goddess, I would shower you with blessings. When I've finished my quest, I'll come back and repay you properly."

Both Benno and Leona stared at her, perplexed, as she gathered her supplies and walked out of the house and down the trail, pausing at each step to catch her breath.

"I don't think she's going to make it, do you?" asked Leona.

"She a goddess, for crying out loud," said Benno under his breath. "Have a little faith."

"What was that?" asked Leona.

"Oh, you heard me, woman," he grunted. "Get back inside."

Chapter Ten

Alzena slept peacefully in the forest while her children slept sound-lessly beside her. Loud rustling woke her up as Cato came crashing in through the undergrowth. She opened her eyes as he entered Lena's hut. Lena opened her eyes as well, but remained silent, hoping the baby wouldn't wake up.

"We've won the battle, but he's done a lot of damage. We have a lot of work to do."

Alzena got to her feet, also grateful Nova had not awakened, and quietly roused Leko. "Come on, Leko, wake up. Your father's here."

Malkin, fast asleep after tending to her burned foot the night before, opened his eyes at the sound of voices. "What's going on?" he asked.

"We got rid of the dragon for now, but we've still got a lot of work to do. Some of the lions are in the process of helping me get the fires put out and assisting the villagers. We need everyone's help this time."

"Well, I'm coming too," said Lena. "I'll bring my herbs for the ones that have been burned. I'm sure there are a lot of them."

The fields of Santara waited at the edge of the forest. As they grew closer, the light began to break through the trees more and more, but a red haze of smoke fouled the color of the light passing through the trees. Alzena was horrified at the damage. Although the dragon had left the forest intact, wide swaths of farmland had been burned. Towers lay in ruins. Houses had been torched as well. She stared at the disaster, help-less. Survivors wandered through the ashes, many of them with burns on their arms that sang across the fields with red soreness and burned like a fire in her belly.

Alzena turned to Margaret. "The children shouldn't have to see this.

Get them to safety. Sir Silve will guard you. Hurry!"

Margaret took Nova, grabbed Leko by the arm, and then Silve led them on a path that would soon take them away from the horrific scene.

Lena looked at a man lying on the ground, burns on his arms already swelling and blistering.

"This one's not too bad," she said. "I can save him. Go help the others."

Alzena looked at the next man on the ground. He was burned so badly that there was no hope. He was already gone, not even breathing. Alzena cut a patch off his tunic so his family could know of his passing. She placed a cloth over his head to provide him some decency in death.

The next man had avoided the fires, but he had a large gash on his forehead from the dragon's talon. The other talon had only nicked his neck, and that wound wouldn't require much attention. But the wound on his head would have to be sealed with intense heat.

Where the wounded had been moved, the occasional fire burned to keep them warm and allow for sealing wounds. Alzena drew her long dagger from her belt and allowed the blade to hover over the fire, warming as the flames licked the cold steel. As the iron heated, it became first red and finally yellow. She knew it was time. The rubies on the hilt took longer to warm and kept her hand cool as she held the yellow-hot dagger.

Alzena knew it would hurt when she closed the wound. She looked for a rag on the ground, but the mud had ruined everything. She grabbed the sleeve of her dress and ripped off a section without thinking twice.

"Here, grab onto this," she said. "It's going to hurt."

The man on the ground quickly bit onto the fabric, breathing faster and faster as the dagger drew closer to his head.

Alzena refused to allow herself one flinch as the knife burned the skin shut on his forehead, the bleeding veins sealed and cooked until the wound no longer threatened his life. Then she withdrew the dagger from the sizzling skin. The man took the fabric out of his mouth and gasped for air, freshly energized and alive.

Lena came over and applied healing paste to his forehead, and the man relaxed. "Thank you," he said before dozing off. Lena and Alzena moved on to the other survivors.

Cato had been finding the men and rallying them, so now there were villagers all around trying to start cleaning up all the damage. Alzena waved to him, and Cato came over, looking concerned.

"Cato! We need to get the survivors to somewhere safe. They'll die out here in the elements. Some of these men need to start getting caravans from the castle."

The other men began drifting away from the village, on their way to get supplies.

Alzena's words caught the attention of a woman waving by her ruined hut.

"I need your help. My daughter's inside. Please hurry, the roof caved in on her! I think she's dead!"

Cato rushed over to the hut, bravely entering the thatched-roof structure even though most of the roof was hanging dangerously from the walls. He searched through the damaged house, discovering the crib in the corner and a small bundle wrapped inside of it. He ran over to the baby, picking the small infant up in his arms. It lay so still, he was sure that it was gone, and her mother's wails outside stirred his soul. He continued to cradle the baby, checking her fragile wrists for any thumping heartbeat.

As he grasped the tiny wrist with his massive hand, the baby awakened and drew in a deep breath.

Before the first lusty cry escaped the infant's lungs, Cato had already left the hut and the baby screamed into the afternoon sky, to be met with peals of laughter and shouts of gratitude from the mother.

Cato handed the baby to its grateful mother, and then looked at Alzena questioningly.

She was happy to advise him. "When you get to the castle, let them know we have refugees coming in. Those extra rooms need to be made ready for guests. They haven't been cleaned in months."

Cato strode over to a nearby horse, and thanks to his close bond with animals, quickly spurred the horse to action. Even after these four long years since the curse had been lifted from his people, the blood of the lions still pumped through his veins from time to time.

Cato returned with many caravans and soon the wounded had been loaded up, followed by those who could still walk, and finally, the whole caravan took off in the direction of the castle. Cato remained behind for a few short minutes, making sure everybody had been evacuated.

After Alzena reached the castle with the survivors, she was still helping them get arranged in a circle in the courtyard, and even after the bowmen began carrying water to the survivors, Alzena carried buckets with them.

Cato arrived a few minutes later, having found no stray villagers, dismounted from his horse, and made an announcement.

"The meeting will commence once we've gathered in the throne room. I'm sure you have a lot of things you need to talk about."

He walked into the castle, and one by one, the villagers began to put away their belongings and file in the throne room.

Alzena heard a commotion rise inside the castle and followed them into the throne room, where everyone was trying to talk at once and Cato was trying to calm them down but not succeeding very well.

"Everyone! Please calm down!"

At the sound of Alzena's voice, the din in the room fell to a low chatter and finally to a silence.

"I know you're very distressed right now, but we have to have order or the king can't listen to you all. Cato, put your staff down in front of the crowd. Only one person can hold it at a time. Then you can all get your turn to talk to Cato. None of you will be taxed for a whole year, and we shall find ways to rebuild your houses. We will make amends for this tragedy."

"Long live the queen!" cried the crowd.

"Now, you can talk to Cato—but only one at a time!"

The first man approached the staff and picked it up. "Cato, so many people are injured, and some have even died. What will be done about the ones we have lost?"

Alzena spoke up, because Cato was at a loss for words, and the question needed to be addressed desperately. Cato smiled at her with relief. "As far as those you have lost, we have nothing but sorrow and pain. We are carving a monument with the names of everyone that died during the attack, which we shall place here at the castle in their memory, beside Queen Lydia's monument. My mother would have loved to see so many people here in the castle. You are welcome to stay as long as you need."

As Alzena walked away, she heard a solitary voice address the king and she smiled peacefully, knowing that order had been restored.

Chapter Eleven

Ilmatar was chilled to the bone from the salt mist that hung in the air near the sea. Every step was a stab of pain from her feet up through her legs.

She stumbled in the fog and would have lost her footing were it not for the walking stick, which she held onto for dear life.

She resumed her footing on the tricky pathway, continuing between rocks and exposed roots of large bushes growing among the dunes.

Even before she could see any landmarks, she heard the haunting melodies of the harps and flutes and drums. These melodies reminded her of the music she had heard from high above Santara, the music that had drawn her here.

Suddenly, she spied the looming rock, and further along, the three-story tavern and way station that featured a red roof. Painted wooden slats glared bright in the late afternoon sun that cut through the mists and beamed down on the shining roof. Horse stalls in the adjacent stable housed many chuffing horses, and she hurried past the stalls to get to the tavern.

It was surprisingly warm inside, and full of laughing men and women. The walls were stone and sloped toward the ceiling, and the tables beneath were covered in glowing candles that changed the color of the stone to a shining red that was exceptionally inviting after her dismal trek.

Some of the patrons were dressed in armor, others in common clothes, but everyone was drinking and making merry. Reindeer blankets covered the seats. The harps played in the corner, and the flutes trilled merrily in harmony. Oval drums pounded out a strong rhythm, while the sacred artwork painted on each drum vibrated with the impact of the carved bone drumsticks. Ilmatar smiled at the musicians that directed her steps to the tavern when she had been lost in the fog.

As the song finished, a spirit of celebration rushed through the tavern and the conversations grew louder as the musicians took a break.

A bowman with long golden hair raised up his mug and cried, "Another round of Sahti!"

The serving girl came out with a huge pitcher of beer and poured everyone large servings.

Ilmatar quickly found a seat. She was handed a drink, which smelled like juniper, but she declined from tasting it immediately. She stared at the men in bold uniforms with bows slung over their shoulders. She was paying particularly close attention to one brown-haired bowman whose hair ran far past his shoulders. He seemed to gather the most respect from his friends, and she realized how much power they had together, and what a good force they would be supporting her on her journey.

She was so caught up with the bowmen that she didn't realize someone had sat down across from her at the table until she gave in and reached for a sip of the juniper beer in the mug. She was astonished to see a lion seated across from her, a lion wearing clothing like any other person in the bar.

This lion was sporting a fantastic mane around his shoulders and up his neck, and his height was at least seven feet tall when he stood up briefly to introduce himself.

"Oh! Did I scare you?"

"No," lied Ilmatar.

As the music started back up, a very pleasant melody, the lion seated in the chair across from her felt more free to speak.

"I couldn't help but notice the smell of blood upon you. I also notice that I've never seen you in this place before. I wonder what brings you here. My friends call me Malkin." As he listened to Ilmatar's response, his nose kept twitching up and down, ever alert, ever smelling his surroundings.

"I don't have very many friends, Malkin. I come from far away, among the reaches of the nebula, and the other gods call me Ilmatar. And yes, my feet are bleeding."

Malkin appeared undisturbed by this statement. Instead, he bowed his head lower than before.

"We have heard so many tales from the bards about the great Ilmatar, Goddess of the Northern Sky. It is my honor to welcome you to Farralina, although I am just passing through. I am on my way to the Land of the Musaat, where I seek inspiration. It is said that the Musaat bring inspiration to anyone who desires it."

"I appreciate the information, and it was very nice to meet you. What I really need is to meet those bowmen, so I can gain transport to Tuonela."

Malkin's eyes widened in astonishment, and his whiskers flickered in terror. "Well, I thank you for telling me that, but I really must be going now. I don't know about the bowmen, but I for one would never dare to venture into the Land of the Dead. I'm far too happy with my life to risk it in a place only the dead call home. I bid you good evening."

At that, the nervous lion picked up his satchel and headed out the door of the tavern, leaving Ilmatar to drink her juniper beer in peace. The warm spices in the drink made her feel much calmer, and drove the chill out of her bones that had lingered from the fog.

The two women getting drunk next to her had overheard Ilmatar, even though she had tried to remain discreet.

The woman with the freckles pointed to her and said, "She's a goddess? If she's a goddess, I'm Queen Alzena!"

Ilmatar kept silent, refusing to be drawn into the conversation.

The man across from her grinned at her, grabbed the waitress from behind, and while she was off balance, gave her behind a good smack. The waitress spilled some of the beer out of the pitcher, and the woman that had been scoffing at Ilmatar scowled and threw her drink at the man. The man shook his head to release the drink from his hair, took another slurp of his own ale, and laughed.

Nearby, a young child watching the interchange howled ferociously.

"This is no place for a child!" A rich woman, dressed in clothes that made it too obvious how wealthy she was, voiced her disapproval, never once taking her hands off her hips.

Incited by the chaos, the bowmen sitting up at the bar got louder than before, and a cheer rose up from the bowman with long brown hair. "We fought back the black dragon! Cato delivered the final blow that drove him back! Three cheers for Cato! Three cheers for the bowmen!"

"Three cheers to Raguel!" shouted another bowman, and everyone lifted their glasses to the brown-haired man.

The men all started cheering and drinking faster than before. Ilmatar took another drink of the juniper beer and set it back down just as another round was placed in front of her by the serving girl, who didn't care how many drinks she gave away as long as they kept disappearing from her tray.

The bowmen continued to rave in the corner. "Cato used the Sword of Light to drive the dragon away!"

As the bowman named Raguel sauntered away from the other bowmen and walked past her table, Ilmatar stood up and grabbed him by the arm, catching his attention.

"I need to find Cato!" Ilmatar hissed.

"It's very easy to find King Cato," laughed Raguel. "He's only the King of all Santara!" The other people in the bar began laughing as well.

"Can you bring me to him right away?" she begged, realizing everyone in the bar was probably staring at her already. "I'm a goddess on a very important mission."

A peal of gasps burst forth in the tavern.

"What's a goddess doing in a tavern? Wait, what do you mean, now? We're trying to have a celebration here."

She noticed that her feet were starting to hurt, and she loosened her grip on his arm as she lost her balance. She grabbed the table quickly, and the bowman helped her to her seat. He sat down in the chair opposite Ilmatar, and starting drinking the second mug of Sahti.

"Your feet are hurting you. You're not used to walking. I'll have to get another horse, but that's never an issue."

"You can help me?" Ilmatar dropped her shoulders in relief. "If this Cato is as great as you say he is, he'll be strong enough to rescue my daughter. She's being held hostage in the Land of the Dead."

"The Land of the Dead is no fit place for a goddess. I will escort you to King Cato, and keep you safe. He's only a day's ride from here. But if we start now, we'll be lost in the forest by nightfall with nowhere to camp safely. I don't want to put a goddess in that kind of danger."

Ilmatar felt insulted that people of Santara kept doubting her strength, but squared her shoulders, and answered, "All right, if we have to spend the night, it's better in the this tavern than in that freezing cold fog."

"That's the smartest thing I've heard you say in the last hour," said Raguel and returned to the other laughing bowmen.

Chapter Twelve

The next morning, she had the distinct pleasure of her first time riding a horse. The brown-haired Raguel presented her with a yellow ribbon.

"Now your hair won't blow in the wind so much. The ribbon belongs to my wife, but she won't mind if a goddess wears it. May I?" He gestured to her hair.

She nodded and turned around, keeping her senses on alert for any threat behind her. The bowman carefully laced her long curling hair through the ribbon until a spiral was formed, a style fit for a queen.

She brushed her new braid over her shoulder to admire it, and while she gazed, Raguel wrapped a heavy green cloak around her shoulders, and she was grateful for the immediate warmth in the cold foggy morning.

"Now you're ready to ride. If you don't mind?"

She nodded, and the bowman helped her ascend to the horse, lacing his strong fingers together so she could step up to the horse's back easily.

"Hold on tight," said the bowman, mounted his own horse, and stirred the grey stallion to action.

The horse started forward, and the rest of the bowmen, and Ilmatar's horse as well, all struck off into the fields of Farralina, on the way to the Forbidden Forest and, beyond that, the heart of the kingdom, Santara.

The prospect of meeting King Cato thrilled her. The king was a man who surely would have the courage to enter Tuonela with her and rescue the young goddess.

The fields were breathtaking, endless expanses of grain and corn as far as she could see. The green blades of grass waved back and forth in the breeze without obstruction, and as they headed inland, the fog cleared, leaving a sunny landscape before her as the grey clouds peeled away and stayed behind them, leaving only sunny meadows. In the distance, hills covered in thick trees told her that she was nearing the forest that stood between her and King Cato.

The smell of the ocean lingered far beyond the fog, and the land had an enchanted quality to it. Small farmhouses dotted the lands.

As they passed through a village, people even came out of the houses to watch them. The houses had thatched roofs that sloped very steeply so the rain would drip away. Sheep covered in white fluff ran past the houses, as well as barking, snapping dogs that lunged around in packs.

Young children hung off the fences, craning for a better view. Older boys ran through the pathways, swinging their fragile swords back and forth in attempts to catch their attention.

One of the youths was exceptionally bad at swordplay, banging his sword into the brick wall surrounding the village so many times that one of the bowmen commented, "Hey, boy, be careful with that thing, or you'll be building the town a new wall!"

Once the boy stopped swinging his sword and retreated, the other boys began to lose interest in the bowmen one by one, as it became clear they were not inviting any new recruits to travel with them today.

The fields were full of flowers blooming in many different colors. As Ilmatar passed by beautiful white flowers that exploded from the stems in long lines of brilliant white petals, she couldn't help but ask her guide what they were called.

"Oh, these are the luscious Bird Cherries," answered Raguel. "They become bright red fruit once the yellow cherry birds come and pollinate them. If you stay here much longer, you'll see them. By next week, they should be all around the valleys, bringing the flowers to fruit so they can eat."

"Why do you let them eat the cherries?"

"The cherry birds are the sacred ambassadors of Milla, the long-lost ruler of Tuonela. Because they still nourish his soul, we let the birds have their fill of the fruit before we harvest. In his honor, these fruits that we may still harvest are called tuomi."

"What a fantastic flower, and what a wonderful story," said Ilmatar.

As they traveled deeper into the lands, the forest grew around them, and when they were deep in the forest, the brown-haired bowman stopped the horses. "The horses are tired. We'll set up camp for the night here."

Ilmatar was surprised by this change of plans. "What do you mean we're stopping here for the night, Raguel? I thought we were meeting Cato today."

"I said days, not one day. The Forbidden Forest is very wide. We'll never cross in a single day, and at night the forest becomes much more dangerous. The horses need water, and they need rest. Besides, it's already late afternoon. Men! Make camp!"

The men began to drift away in pairs, using their shared strength to raise up tents.

Other bowmen drifted into the forest, roaming for food. The lead bowman pulled a long blanket from his horse pack and unrolled the blanket across the grass. "Lady, your feet need attention. Take off your shoes and I can take care of you. That's your tent they're setting up right over there."

Ilmatar looked at the tent. At the moment, it was a pile of long branches arranged in a pyramid. By looking around, Ilmatar could see other tents already completed, with hides wrapped around the poles to keep out the cold wind.

Fires had been started inside some of them already, and white smoke was foaming out of the tops. The smell of wood smoke was very pleasant to her, for as a goddess floating above Santara, many times she had smelled the wonderful smoke and the frying fish and woodland creatures, and had been enticed almost as much by the aromas as she had by the harp music that had finally convinced her to come to Santara.

Ilmatar had a sensation that the great circle was starting to bond together, and she felt a deep sense of calm and tranquility. She felt safe among these tents, and feeling safe, felt willing to leave her perch on the horse.

When she dismounted, her feet hit the ground hard, and she cried out in pain.

"Let me help you," said Raguel.

The bowman helped her over to the tree by the blanket, and she leaned back against it, moaning in pain.

The bowman tried to help her remove her shoes, but even that was excruciating. Her feet had become swollen and blistered in the heat of the

ride, and bouncing up and down from the moving horse had added
bruises to her ankles. The shoes no longer fit well at all, but constricted
her feet and made the pain worse. Raguel pulled the shoe, and the bark
scraped against her skin and caused more pain. She cried out and reached
out her arms in supplication.

"Stop!" she cried. "It hurts too much!"

"I know a lot of things about the herbs in the forest," said Raguel.
"My mother taught me everything she knew about nature. I know many
different healing herbs that grow down near the river."

"Your mother sounds like a very wise woman, Raguel. You should go
gather those herbs."

Ilmatar spent her time alone carefully peeling back the bark shoes until her feet were finally free.

By that time, Raguel had returned with several different herbs piled
into his basket. Ilmatar stared at them suspiciously, having never seen
them before. He rolled a blanket out on the floor.

"There, lay down on the blanket."

Ilmatar was about to follow his command when suddenly Ukko
came down over the treetops, with his face almost kissing the tops of the
trees, and hung above the bowmen and Ilmatar.

Raguel ran to his horse and grabbed his bow. Notching an arrow, he
aimed his bow at the massive face hanging above him.

With a soft breath of air sent down from his lips, Ukko blew on Ilmatar's feet. Ilmatar felt the healing begin instantly. The bowman was
holding on to the bow, but helplessly watched it rip out of his hands and
get blown into the woods by the powerful wind. Ilmatar looked down
and saw that her feet were completely healed. She looked back up at her
brother, and the blowing wind stopped.

The bowmen took advantage of the quiet to aim their arrows at
Ukko's face far above.

Ilmatar got to her feet, shocked that there was no pain at all, no cuts
or scrapes, but that her brother had completely healed her. She cried out
and threw up her hands to draw attention.

"Stop!"

The bowmen lowered their weapons at once.

"What are you doing? That's a god you're trying to shoot, and he's not just any god; he's my mean, dangerous, vicious brother, Ukko, God of the Thunderclouds, and he's just come down here to heal my feet! And what's more, he's done a much better job than the lot of you!"

The bowmen dropped their bows and fell to their knees before Ukko.

"Hey!" Ilmatar cried out to Ukko. "How come you can come down here whenever you want and I have to stay down here?"

"I'm much stronger than you," he answered, and the power of his breath stirred the branches of the trees. Ukko smiled down at the bowmen and his sister. "Keep her safe," he said firmly.

Even those three strong words stirred the air violently, and leaves began flying through the air. The bowmen had to clutch their bows to themselves to keep them from being blown away again. Ukko saw the effects of his words, and tried to stifle a laugh, realizing that it would be disastrous.

Ukko started backing away, but when he got to a safe distance in the air, he started laughing loudly.

Realizing that Ilmatar was indeed a goddess, the bowmen began bowing down to her. Ilmatar stared at them, let them kneel for a few long seconds, and then quietly shuffled her hands to compel them to rise.

"Enough sitting around! We are on a mission! Besides, it's barely past noon yet. Look at the sun! That was just Ukko's shadow making it dark. Let's get moving!"

Wordlessly, the whole battalion of bowmen got back on their horses. Ilmatar got back on her horse without any trouble at all, whistling past its ribs with her bare feet, and landing light as a feather. She found that her bare toes gave her much better traction than the smooth bark shoes.

"Forward," cried Ilmatar.

The brown-haired bowman flinched.

"I'm supposed to say that," he complained.

"Silence!" commanded Ilmatar.

The bowmen continued through the forest in silence. Ilmatar enjoyed the birds singing in the trees as they continued through the woods.

Chapter Thirteen

Ilmatar was so much happier with the silence in the woods.

"Where are we?" she asked.

The trees were full of singing birds. The smell in the air was fantastic. She felt like she'd been granted access to a paradise— Ilmatar, who not so long ago had been a goddess herself, free to roam the giant nebula and the vast galaxies beyond.

"The Forbidden Forest, my goddess," said the bowman. "Soon we'll be nearing the fields of Santara."

"Why do they call it the Forbidden Forest if we're traveling through it?" asked Ilmatar.

"My lady, not so long ago, men were cursed to become lions every night and exiled to this jungle. The brave Cato you seek was one of the Lion-People before he broke the curse and set his people free. No one has taken the time to give this magnificent forest a new name."

As they passed through the stately trees, with frogs croaking in the ferns and loons whooping by the ponds, Ilmatar felt as though the forest was enchanted, not forbidden.

"They must have had such a wonderful life here," mused Ilmatar. Remembering Malkin, she could imagine the Lion-People living in these woods.

"Much has changed since then. These woods are empty of people now, other than a race of true lion-men who still live in a distant village. They are far behind us, my goddess."

Ilmatar continued through the forest, contemplating the singing birds and fantastic flowers.

As they broke through the trees, endless fields of grains embraced the bowmen and Ilmatar in a warm golden glow. But she could see the damage done by the black dragon. She realized the tantalizing smell in the air was the smoke from these fires as they smoldered, dampened but not completely out yet.

In the distance, a tower hung to one side, toppled by its fiery breath. The beams were already burnt to a crisp, blackened and useless, and the tower cage hung abandoned and desolate.

Between her and the magnificent castle, fields had been burned and stood in blackened circles. Even here by the forest, some of the wooden houses had been burned, but those that stood were quaint and rustic. They perched with towering roofs to cast the winter snow aside, and rounded stables that had escaped the dragon's wrath held more horses and farm animals.

"The great farmlands of Santara," said Raguel. "This is the reason why Santara is always overflowing with wealth and good fortune. These crops are the lifeblood of the kingdom. The dragon destroyed the lives of these poor farmers when he blazed through here. Profits will only arrive if much work takes place."

Surveying the damage slowly on horseback, she wondered how anyone could stop a fire-breathing beast single-handedly.

Raguel spoke further. "This one brave man, Seppo, was able to escape the burning village as the dragon set it ablaze. Thanks to Seppo, word got to the lions, and they alerted King Cato. Cato fought the dragon bravely, but the dragon killed three people at the castle, and six more in this village. But he saved many villages from destruction. If it weren't for Seppo and Malkin, this would have been looking far worse. Nevertheless, Seppo's village was destroyed, so the villagers were invited into the castle. I've heard the castle is bustling right now. It has many, many rooms, but there are many refugees."

Ilmatar could already see, even from this distance, that the castle indeed possessed hundreds of rooms, each with tall windows to allow the light in, and magnificent towers.

The castle continued to command her attention as they approached, and she stopped listening even though Raguel continued talking. Miles away, she could already see the fine battlements, and the walkways high above for the watchmen.

A huge flag with a blue cross flew above the battlements, and she couldn't help but feel welcome in this wonderful kingdom.

The whole party stopped before the gates. The royal trumpets sounded loudly, and none of the bowmen moved until the fanfare died away.

Two guards stood before massive wooden doors. She was amazed at the height of the doors, to allow war machines in and out, she presumed, and the fine designs on the massive hinges. At the end of the fanfare, the guards approached the bowmen.

"You are the bowmen, this I can plainly see. You may pass. But who is this woman you bring with you, and where did you get the horse?"

"Enough, Lanne! This woman has a critical message for King Cato. We're going through here even if we have to go right through you."

"I think you've made your point, Raguel. You all may pass. Ladies first," he said with a smile, gesturing the direction with his arm.

Since Ilmatar could clearly see the gate, she ignored his insult and headed to the gate.

The bowmen stood aside while Ilmatar walked past the guard to the gate. The second guard opened a smaller door inside. The smaller door surprised Ilmatar, as she had seen no trace of it on the way across the bridge.

The bowmen quickly followed Ilmatar into the castle courtyard.

Once inside, a young boy in his teens ran up and began to grab the reins of the horses as the bowmen dismounted. The men ignored the stable boy and continued on their way to the castle, talking about getting drunk.

Ilmatar was more polite and smiled kindly at the young man as he grabbed the reins of her horse, and she easily dismounted, breathing a deep sigh of relief as her feet hit the stone walkways of the courtyard without even a sting of pain.

Refugees and soldiers milled around the courtyard, some going about their business, others lounging and eating. To Ilmatar it was a magical sight after floating through the lonely nebula with nobody but the other gods for company, and then hundreds of years in the ocean with her closest friends, the musical Nakki, to find a group of people all around her and no shortage of people to talk to. Then she remembered she needed to talk to King Cato, and started wandering through the people, trying to find him. People with crowns should be easy to spot, she reasoned.

Chapter Fourteen

Massive trees stood within the fine courtyard. Ilmatar was overwhelmed with the grandeur since nothing ever grew in the turbulent plasmas and clouds of the nebula. She gazed at the magnificent trees, resting her eyes on each one before moving on to the next, each taller than her body when she had been a goddess.

Her eyes floated from tree to tree until she suddenly noticed a woman with a very subtle crown perched on her head, staring at a tall statue of a fair woman resting in the courtyard next to a small stone plaque. A young boy stayed close behind her, and a baby nestled in her arms.

Ilmatar approached the queen from the side so she would see her, and politely said, "Your Highness," noticing that many people addressed royalty this way on Santara.

Alzena looked surprised at the introduction and shook her head. "My name is Alzena. I happen to be the queen in this castle, but I have always been Alzena, and I will always stay Alzena. Allow me to bid you welcome to Cato's castle."

"If you are the queen of Cato's castle, then where is King Cato? I am Ilmatar, the goddess. I have been told to speak with him."

"Then you are the one the bowmen asked me to find," answered Alzena. "Cato reminded the bowmen that he's conducting a meeting, and they came to find me instead."

"I asked for King Cato," responded Ilmatar. "He's the one that lifted the curse. I need someone with his strength to help me. I was a goddess once, but now I'm just a mortal called Ilmatar. If I'm going to survive a journey to the Land of the Dead, I need to have someone very courageous to lead the voyage."

Alzena looked at Ilmatar with frustration. "Well, he may have lifted the curse, but I'm the one who gave him the map. He'd still be turning into a wild animal every night if it wasn't for me! If you want courageous, you should stop looking right now."

Ilmatar nodded wisely. "Don't let me be the one to doubt your capabilities, Alzena. I've always supported all the women of Santara."

"According to the legends, no one's seen you for almost eight hundred years. That means you haven't helped anybody in centuries. What happened to you?" asked Alzena.

"I was busy bringing a new goddess into the world, Loviatar the goddess of Ocean and Sky combined. But she was captured and taken to Tuonela, and now I'm on a quest to free her."

"It sounds like you need my help, too," said Alzena. "Last time the king didn't take me on the quest, it almost got him killed. This time there's no way he's taking off unless I can keep an eye on him while he's traveling."

Ilmatar nodded. "You're more than welcome to come along. I'm sure we could use all the help we can get. By the way, what is this statue you were looking at?"

"A monument to my mother, Queen Lydia. After my father died, she just wasn't the same. She was still Queen of Santara, but her heart died the day my father did. Within a year, she was gone. Even the royal physicians declared that she died of a broken heart."

"I'm so sorry for your loss."

Alzena smiled and raised her hand in protest. "All is forgiven. You are still a goddess in my eyes. How can we help you?"

"I need a boat to take me to the Land of the Dead, and I'm sure one the royal ships is strong enough to survive the journey. Can you talk to King Cato about this? I would be so grateful for your help. When I complete my quest, I can become a goddess again. I promise you, on behalf of your entire kingdom, that no one in this land will want for anything again if you can help me."

Alzena sighed. "The king is a very busy man, but I can listen to your problems. As you can see, there's been a dragon attack, and things are in chaos, but when the lives of gods are at stake, I wouldn't dare to stand in the way. Let me get you a room so we can sit and talk. We need to get you cleaned up after the long journey. Do you think my dress would fit you? You look like you're about my size."

Ilmatar looked down at her clothes ruefully. "Yes, they should fit fine, thank you," she said. "We have much to discuss."

"Let's get inside. I'm sure you're desperate to see civilization after so many days on the road."

Alzena went into the castle, followed by Ilmatar, and whisked her into one of the rooms. It was unoccupied, but it was already fitted with a massive bed, and even more importantly, a pool of hot water embedded in the floor, and a mirror for makeup. She was amazed by these new surroundings. The bathing area was magnificent, with marble shining through the water and two marvelous statues of goddesses around the rim.

"That would be the Goddess of Light, wouldn't it?" Ilmatar pointed to the second statue. "This sculpture would be the Goddess of Fire."

"Fantastic," said Alzena.

"I was good friends with them," said Ilmatar. "Before they came here to Santara. I haven't seen them lately."

"I'm privileged to welcome a goddess to the castle. Please make yourself feel at home."

Ilmatar had a fine palace in the nebula, but here on Santara, the royal guests enjoyed a whole table of delicacies, flowers in vases that would never grow in the nebula, and so much more.

"Alzena, this room is wonderful! If all the rooms in the castle are like this, every guest must feel like royalty. This place is better than my own palace."

"Margaret!" Alzena cried.

Ilmatar looked toward the door. The portly nurse walked in. "Yes?"

"This is Ilmatar. Could you please see that she gets a good bath? She's been on the road for a long time."

"Absolutely, Queen Alzena."

"Oh, Margaret, one more thing. Before you do that, would you go to my chambers and get that yellow dress and that red dress? I would so much like our guest to have some decent clothes."

"Right away," said Margaret.

"I'd better get going," said Alzena.

The bath was very warm, and Ilmatar was extremely happy with the new experience. When she emerged, she was completely clean, and the yellow dress Alzena had given her fit perfectly. She felt completely different walking back down to the garden, more at peace and more civilized and refined. Although she had enjoyed her voyage through the countryside, she enjoyed life in the castle far more.

Once she was ready, she walked down the corridor to the garden. She was grateful that Alzena had found her a room so close to the garden, because the palace was so big she feared she would get lost otherwise.

Alzena was waiting in the garden for her, and motioned her over to the bench. Ilmatar sat down softly.

"Now just wait here for a few minutes, and I'll go get Cato. I heard the advisors arguing a few minutes ago, but I'm sure they're almost done by now. They've been in there talking since last night, so they had better be done soon!" Alzena waved to Margaret as she bustled through the courtyard. "Margaret! Could you please take care of Leko for a little while? I need to have a private meeting. In fact, since I'm almost certainly leaving on a journey tomorrow, would you mind looking out for Leko and Nova until I get back?"

"Whatever you say, Alzena. I'll look out for him, that's for sure."

"What's that supposed to mean?" laughed Alzena.

The nurse shot her a look of scorn. "He listens to me very good, which is more than I can ever say about you, young lady!" Then she headed off into the castle proper through the kitchen as the young boy was pulling her in the direction of the aromas and vigorously rubbing his belly with his free hand.

Ilmatar looked at the baby. "What about her?"

"Oh, Nova will be fine. She loves meeting new friends. Margaret may be our nursemaid here, but she's not that great with the babies. Now Lena, Cato's mother, just made it to the castle yesterday. She's incredibly good with children. I think I shall let Lena take care of her while I'm gone."

The baby smiled deeply at Ilmatar. Ilmatar blushed at the power of insight in the young baby as she bowed reflexively. Even though she was upside down, looking up at Ilmatar from her mother's arms, she still lifted her head and pulled it forward, putting her hands together at the same time.

"She knows you used to be a goddess. She's too smart for her baby blanket, she is."

Ilmatar was enraptured by the tiny bundle in Alzena's hands with the puff of hair hanging like a cloud over her head.

The garden was more fantastic than the courtyard. Surrounded by high walls so even the wild deer could not break through, it was a peaceful place. Nobody visited, either through boredom or sheer ignorance. It was abandoned other than the gardener, who was just finishing raking the weeds and was on his way out.

"Stay here," said Alzena. "I'll get Cato for you."

The baby cried out, waving at Ilmatar.

"I think she likes you. On second thought, why don't you hold on to her while I go and get Cato? The throne room is no place for a baby."

"Sure," said Ilmatar, trying to hide the astonishment on her face. Never before had she gotten to hold a little baby in her arms, and the tiny creature now nestled against her reminded her of her own little baby, so far away and unprotected.

She reflected on how she had never been able to hold her own daughter, and the feeling of dread began to swim around her mind as she imagined never seeing Loviatar again.

Ilmatar lost sense of time as she watched over the small baby, who gently held onto her finger and burped occasionally. The more she watched her, the more she could focus on the small creature and forget about her own child. In this way, Ilmatar spent her time alone in the garden in a state of bliss.

Chapter Fifteen

Alzena squared her shoulders as she prepared to enter the throne room. She could already tell that King Cato was still busy.

The din of the voices inside still rose up and wafted through the corridors of the castle, where Alzena tried to steel her nerves, but grew tenser by the second instead.

She bravely marched into the room, knowing the will of the gods and goddesses was more important than the needs of some villagers, even if they were her subjects. She heard her teachers advising her in her mind, telling her that to turn away from the Divine was to turn to the ways of evil.

The farmers were busy arguing with the advisors and King Cato. The advisors were looking very nervous. Cato was looking very tired with his head supported by his hand, his elbow resting on the arm of his magnificent throne, glowering at the farmers as they continued to argue.

Alzena knew the king was supposed to support the throne, not the other way around. She breathed deeply, pleading for patience as she suppressed the urge to speak up immediately in defense of her exhausted husband.

Another farmer spoke up, desperate for help. "We have lost so many fields to the fires! We need at least a hundred bushels of seed to replant!"

"Isn't it more important," said an advisor, "to focus on the black dragon, Sire, and find a way to stop it from coming back? We can't lose any more farms or we'll go hungry."

Cato raised his hand. "We discussed this. The Goddess of Light created a magic barrier around the castle after the dragon attack. The dragon won't get through again."

"But Sire, how do we know it's going to hold?" One of the women spoke up this time, with an added chorus of cries from the other women.

Alzena began to recognize panic on some of the faces in the crowd and knew she had to act soon.

Before she could address the panicking crowd, one of the king's advisors lost his temper and stole the moment away from her, venting his frustration from a face turned red with fury.

"That's not the matter at hand here! It's the farms we need to focus on! You'll get your seeds, just like I promised you! Let me take care of one thing at a time! I can't do this anymore!"

The advisor stormed out of the room, and the farmer tried to speak up, but Alzena raised her hand and the farmer closed his mouth firmly. Once the advisor had taken his aggression out of the throne room, Alzena felt the tension decrease tremendously, and she was able to breathe a sigh of relief before she addressed the crowd.

"Thank you," she said. "Cato, have you reached a conclusion yet? There's a goddess outside that wants to talk with you."

Cato stared back at her from the throne. His face was tired and aging. Even though Cato was fully human now, traces of golden hair around his eyes revealed that he had once been a regal lion.

Fine decorations of solid gold graced Cato's robes, for the kingdom had enjoyed good harvests for years. His beard had grown back out and now hung, braided with blue ribbons, the color of Santara, down to his knees as he hunched on the throne.

"All right, everyone, I have other matters to attend to. Please clear the room. We'll meet tomorrow morning. I'll have grain for everyone. Please take your leave."

The farmer spoke up. "But, my king, what about that dragon?"

"We've been discussing this since yesterday!" roared Cato, loud enough to echo through the chamber and leave the farmer staring terrified at him. "Arguing and arguing and arguing and arguing! I can't take it anymore! I've got other things to take care of! Go back to your rooms and try to get some sleep! Okay?"

Everyone was staring wide-eyed at Cato now. One by one, they began to leave their places and start heading for the door, watching Cato the whole time.

As the room emptied, Cato rose and walked towards Alzena and the exit. "Who is this goddess, my love?" he asked graciously, taking her by the hand and smiling deeply. Unlike his subjects, who were constantly bothering him, he was able to be more relaxed around Alzena, because he knew she loved him far more than any of his subjects ever could. She was the only one who really understood him.

"Her name is Ilmatar. I read about her long ago, when I was studying the old writing. She was a goddess of the sky, but now she's human and sitting in our garden. She wanted to talk to you as well, but don't think I'll be staying behind on this adventure."

"Didn't she disappear hundreds of years ago?" asked Cato.

"Nobody's heard from her in hundreds of years, but I'm sure the gods and goddesses have their own reasons for what they do."

"Exactly what is a goddess doing in our garden?"

"Goddesses don't just take on human form for any reason. It has to be something serious if she's had to take drastic measures."

"Well, let's see what's going on. Where have you been all day anyway? I could have used your help."

"I was talking to my mother for advice, and then the goddess came along," answered Alzena.

"I think you should be asking this goddess for advice," answered Cato. "Goddesses are very wise, and if one of them took the time to talk with you, you should feel very blessed."

"I do feel blessed, but I wish she wouldn't think so highly of you. She wouldn't rest until I promised her I would bring you to see her."

"I'll have to take that as a compliment," said Cato.

"You'd better," Alzena shot back.

"Exactly. You're twice as brave as I am, but she'll find that out soon enough."

They exited the castle, both smiling from ear to ear, and went to the garden. Cato and Alzena had learned from many years of negotiation that being positive during an important meeting was the most important factor in a successful interchange.

"She's holding our daughter. You must really trust her."

"Cato, really?"

"Sorry," he replied, although neither of their smiles disappeared for a second.

Margaret returned and picked up the little baby.

Cato sat down with Ilmatar and Alzena in the garden. "Tell us your story, goddess. What need does a goddess have of me?"

"I was a great goddess of the sky, but I fell to Santara and became one with the ocean spirits. I carried a child to birth, but she was stolen from me before I could even hold her in my arms."

Cato was shocked by the tale. "Who has the audacity to steal a goddess?"

"At first I thought it was my brother Ukko, but he saved me, too late for my daughter. My brother said that the wizard I'm after is called Tursas because he wields the plumes of ink beneath the sea, and the fire in the sky, just like the evil forces that stole my baby. I know that he dwells in the Land of the Dead."

Alzena raised her eyebrows in surprise, raising her hand to politely stop Ilmatar. "I have many books and scrolls about the Land of the Dead," she interjected. "We have a fine collection of scrolls in our library."

"Well, let's get over there then!" cried Ilmatar. "The sooner I can reach the Land of the Dead and save my daughter, the sooner I can get back to being a goddess."

They all stood up and headed into the castle. Now Ilmatar was smiling. For the first time since the plumes of darkness had stolen her daughter away, she felt hope and realized the power of emotion as excitement and happiness tickled her arms and pushed her to grin in spite of all the dangers she was willingly headed into.

Chapter Sixteen

Ilmatar was surprised when they started heading down the spiral staircase. "Who keeps all their treasured writings underground? Shouldn't they be high up in the towers, for all the world to see their knowledge?"

Alzena explained as she descended. "These books and scrolls are thousands of years old. Some of these date back to the first people who lived here, who spoke of the first cities. If they were up in the towers, the elements would destroy them. They are kept preserved down here by the cool, dry air."

As she opened the great oak doors protecting the library, Ilmatar gasped in wonder at the incredible collection of knowledge inside.

The library was splendid, with row after row of stone bookshelves marching back into the shadows. Candles hung from chandeliers high above the books, where even the sparks falling from the candles would be extinguished and cold before they reached the bookshelves. Wood blocks engraved with different subjects defined each section. Alzena read them off as she went down the rows of bookshelves.

"Fruits and berries," she read. "Have you tasted cloudberries? They're the best fruit in the whole world! Animals—we have the biggest birds you've ever seen right here in Santara. Potions, spells—this is almost where we want to be, but spells are really dangerous. I wouldn't mess with them if I were you. Oh, here we go!"

Alzena stopped by a bookcase with the etched block at the end detailing a single strange word. Ilmatar read it aloud carefully. "Tuonela—the Land of the Dead."

"Let me take a look." She pulled a well-worn tome from the bookshelf and opened it. "This book speaks of the Land of the Dead, far out to sea, according to this map. I'm bringing this page with us. We will definitely be needing a map. It says Tuonela is a realm of dragons. Long ago, the dragons were sent to the Land of the Dead as punishment for their dangerous deeds. But it doesn't say anything about Tursas. Let me keep looking."

Alzena pulled another book off the great stone bookshelf, and after turning a few pages, came to another description.

"The Land of the Dead reaches far beyond the Lair of the Dragons, to the Great Endless, a desert where no soul can endure… This book looks promising." Alzena pulled a fourth book from the shelf, paging through it before finding something important and reading aloud. "When Tursas took command of the dragons, he flew them into Tuonela, storming the Land of the Dead. Even Milla's magic and Andri's spiritual powers could not stop him."

"What are you saying?" Ilmatar asked. "The great Milla and Andri are no longer in command? I knew them before they descended here thousands of years ago. They were the most powerful magicians in the Sky Kingdom. That's why they were sent to guard the Land of the Dead in the first place. What could have possibly happened to remove a god and a goddess from power at the same time?"

Alzena nodded, eyes wide with curiosity. "The dragons overwhelmed the rightful rulers of Tuonela, and once they were overthrown, Tursas turned them into dragons. Tursas took command of the Land of the Dead for himself. He used the dragons' power to satisfy his every whim. When the dragons did not serve any purpose for Tursas, he left them for dead in the Graveyard of the Dragons. He locked them in so they would starve to death."

Ilmatar turned to Cato in shock, but restrained her throat from crying out in the quiet library. "He's been killing gods, Cato. If he's powerful enough to end the life of a god, we don't stand a chance."

"When have we ever let danger stop us? Someone like that has to be stopped. People have been telling me all my life I can't do things. I've always proved them wrong. We're not going to let this wizard stop us."

Alzena nodded in agreement. "Once you've dragged your mind back from a crushing, ink-black prison, it takes quite a bit to shake you up, Ilmatar. Don't worry about us."

As Alzena pulled another book from the shelf, a deep crashing sound emerged. Suddenly the stone bookshelf began to crumble under the books, where they collapsed and fell behind the bookshelf, between the wall and the shelves.

"This library is falling apart. We need new stone slabs in here. That dragon attack did more damage than I thought." She combed through the wreckage, trying to clear the biggest pieces of stone from the books below, when she paused and looked behind the bookshelf. "Hold on! I see other scrolls down here. Cato! Can you help me retrieve them? Your arms are a lot longer than mine."

Cato reached far behind the bookshelf, pushing the stones out of the way with his big hands, and finally extracted the ancient scrolls.

Alzena began looking through them, rolling them out on the table and finding something right away on the first scroll. She set the rest of them aside and started reading.

"The Land of the Dead used to be the Land of the Dragons. But long ago, Tursas took over their domain and began enslaving the dragons. His magic was so dark that the land became a portal to the Great Endless, but this scroll says that in ancient times, it was a natural grotto, or sea-cave, and sacred to the Sea God."

Ilmatar asked, "What did he do to the dragons?"

Alzena opened more scrolls, finally finding the next part of the story.

"He turned them into people, enslaving them and binding them to his will. Those he could not bend, he left as dragons, but condemned them to be wardens of this dark land he now possessed. It says here that the dark power of his realm forced him to start abducting the gods themselves, kidnapping them and consuming them for his own powers. The black dragon is the creation of a god and the twisted magic Tursas wields. I think your daughter has become the black dragon, Ilmatar. This scroll was written by one of the wisest poets to ever walk upon this land. It seems we were destined to find this manuscript."

Ilmatar began to shake. "If he's turned my daughter into a horrible dragon, then all is lost. How will I ever get her back?"

"Let's see. Black dragon…black dragon…oh, lifting the curse, here we go. The last scroll in the pile, doesn't that make sense," said Alzena. She read the scroll to herself before she began to read aloud, trying to digest the ancient information. Ilmatar was glad that Alzena was around. She was incapable of reading the ancient runes, even though she had been a goddess not too long ago. As a mortal, that power was gone from her completely, and she was reliant on Alzena and Cato to read the documents for her. The runes looked far more detailed than the modern writing she saw displayed on some of the buildings of Santara and Farralina. Even when it came to the local signs, it was still something she was getting used to.

"It says that even the black dragon has a heart. If that heart can be pierced, then the horrible magic will be destroyed and Tursas will have lost his weapon. Every time he wields a black dragon, the creature terrorizes the farms and villages. That's why we need to stop this menace as soon as possible!"

"So now you agree with me," said Ilmatar. "How soon can you be ready to sail?"

"Tomorrow," answered Alzena. "The royal ship can take you anywhere you need to go."

"I need to talk to some people before I go," Cato said. "I'll see you in the morning. I need to talk to the sailors too. I don't think I'm going to get much sleep tonight. You and Alzena should keep yourselves in the castle tonight. With a dragon on the loose, it's the safest place right now."

"It's true, Ilmatar," Alzena reassured her. "No one was slain here at the castle during the dragon attack."

Cato left the castle, venturing to an isolated glade to pray to the Goddess of Light in private. Valo descended and stood before him, reading his mind before he could open his lips.

"You are going to the Land of the Dead, Cato. I am a creature of light, and cannot follow you to such a horrible place. Neither can any of my holy sisters. You must go there unaided."

Cato bowed. "But I may bring other mortals with me?"

"You may bring as many mortals as you wish, but the Divine must remain outside the realm of Tuonela."

Cato was getting nervous at the prospect of visiting the Land of the Dead without any help from the holy protectors of Santara and the rest of the universe. "This is a dangerous place I'm going. Is there any way you can protect me if you can't come into Tuonela yourself?" asked Cato.

"I can offer you protection, so your soul is not consumed by the evil Tursas, and I will make sure your companions are equally protected. I also have a powerful potion here that will cause great distraction among the evil creatures you will battle when you release it."

"Are you sure I will prevail?" asked Cato.

"My spells will keep your soul brimming with light and peace and tranquility. You have nothing to fear as long as my protection remains. Your own doubt is the only thing that can stop you now, Cato. Doubt is toxic to hope. Extinguish doubt at the first crawling sign."

She vanished before his eyes, leaving Cato with a sense of tranquility. His doubts erased, he traveled to town to rally the sailors and the cook and everyone else he wanted to accompany him on his voyage. Now that the gods were out of the picture, he wanted as many strong souls by his side as possible as he ventured into the Land of the Dead. He wisely kept the destination a total secret from all the sailors.

Chapter Seventeen

Ilmatar thought she'd been accustomed to the sea after hundreds of years in the waters, but the harbor of Santara took her breath away with its beauty. Once she had been a Sky Goddess, and the sea had been her home. Now that she was human, she could easily drown, and her tiny, frail body would disappear into the depths.

Ilmatar sat down on the stones laid beside the path, catching her breath and thinking about her new mortality. The ocean spread out before her in magnificent splendor. Her fear of drowning began to disappear as the enchanting view of the ocean captivated her attention, growing brighter and brighter as her eyes became dazzled.

Every wave caught the sunlight and bounced bright triangles of light back into the air until the surface of the water was literally glowing.

The sea of fire extended beyond the horizon, disappearing into the gray fog that lingered at its edge and drawing her eye further. The hot sun hung above the veil of light, a small star lost above the scintillating waves.

Ilmatar noticed that her breathlessness was not just from the view or her mortality. She realized she was feeling anxious to the point of panic about this journey to Tuonela. On the other side of that bright water rested a place that every mortal dreaded, except for Cato and Alzena, and even then she wondered if they did not harbor some secret unease deep inside their hearts as well.

From her vantage point, Ilmatar could clearly see the ship that would take her to Tuonela. The great ship lay in the harbor, tied to the dock and ready to sail. It was massive and strong, and the huge blue sails towered high above the decks, with the white swans in the center bearing the symbol of Santara across the waves. Men shouted on the deck, fear making their voices higher than normal, so they soared across the harbor and hit her ears clear as day. Strong boards sank beneath the waves, telling of the deep hull beneath.

But how, argued her mind, could mortal bodies stand against this demon Tursas, when she had failed even as a goddess to defeat him?

Ilmatar forced herself to calm down, realizing she was being irrational and acting too human. She pushed her shoulders back, proud of her divine nature, and confident in her ability to defeat this evil with heroes as powerful as Cato and Alzena by her side. She rode on this wave of confidence, and it was strong enough to bring swift energy to her steps.

Cato and Alzena, and many of the sailors who would fight beside them, were already at the ship by the time she made it down to the docks.

"What took you so long?" asked Cato. "I thought you wanted to get going as soon as possible. We've been preparing the *Urwind* ever since the sun came up."

Ilmatar stood boldly on the deck of the *Urwind*, as sailors bustled around, tying down the corners of the sails while others scrubbed the deck and made it shipshape.

King Cato and Queen Alzena ascended the stairs to the wheel, and Ilmatar followed them. "Last call!" cried Cato.

"All aboard!" cried the commander.

Ilmatar noticed a gleaming red ruby shining on Alzena's belt. "That's an amazing ruby—" She stopped herself as Alzena drew a magnificent dagger from her belt, longer than her forearm and sharp enough to gleam in the morning sun. The three of them stood at the wheel, independent from the sailors.

"We travel east, to where the sun rises, and the portal to Tuonela awaits." Cato pulled his weapon out of his belt as well. At the moment, his prized weapon bore the form of the Sword of Light.

Ilmatar raised both palms empty and said, "I might be unarmed, but I have my brother Ukko to help me."

"He can only help you until we reach the Land of the Dead. Valo told me yesterday none of the Divine may enter Tuonela."

"Precisely. Which is why my brother Ukko has made me human. He knew I was going to rescue my daughter, and he wasn't going to stand in my way."

"Well, I'm glad you've got his help until then. Alzena says there are many dangers blocking the way to our destination. She said it's designed to keep out the living. I hope we can make it there in one piece."

Alzena looked around the deck, proud of the work the crew had done. "Everything looks ready. Stop trying to scare the goddess and let's get going already!"

Cato grabbed the wheel, ready to set sail. "Weigh the anchor! Drop the sail! It's time to head to sea!"

Ilmatar felt a rush of excitement she'd never felt before as the mighty ship caught the wind and danced through the water, pulling everyone forward to destiny.

The force of the wind tugging on the sails was so mighty she could feel the wood planks swinging beneath her feet as they shot through the water. The hull groaned and creaked.

Ilmatar realized the creaking was something she would have to get used to, for no matter how long the ship remained on the waves, it continued to creak and moan as the ocean waves continued to crash against it.

The sounds became a sort of background music to her ears, fading into the crying of seagulls and waves cresting and hissing and returning to silent swells.

The safety of the harbor lay behind her, and the welcome of the open ocean lay before her. The ocean had welcomed her to Santara, drew her from the nebula, and nurtured her until she gave life to a daughter of the sea and sky. But now, this goddess had become a mortal, a mortal who evidently could drown or burn. The sea surrounded them and the distant shore became a memory as the hills of Santara disappeared and the ocean swallowed them.

Now she was at the mercy of the *Urwind*, and sailing towards the Land of the Dead. She had begun to comprehend, as she passed the dead bodies still lying in the fields from the dragon's recent attacks, that mortals could very much die, and unlike a goddess or god, could do so very easily.

Chapter Eighteen

As evening fell, a red glow hovered over the horizon, and soon clouds billowed up and a storm arose. The wind blew against the ship's passage, and Cato had to turn the ship to the side to avoid the worst of the storm. All across the horizon, thick dark clouds loomed tall and massive in the sky. High above the thunderclouds, sprites flashed near the edge of the atmosphere where it merged with the nebula.

Beneath the purple sprites flashing above the clouds, bright bolts of lightning raced.

Rain poured down from the sky until the boat and the sails were completely soaked. The winds blew stronger and stronger, and the swells turned to waves. The waves grew worse as the hours dragged on, making it harder to hold the mainsail steady.

As the hours dragged on and sunrise seemed like it would never come, the waves began to crash over the deck. Sailors clung to the ropes for dear life as the water washed across the deck like a river.

Even Ilmatar had difficulty holding on, and though she begged for relief from the gods, nothing happened.

The storm continued to pound, unabated. Between the surges, sailors would run across the deck to the other ropes, trying to hold fast to the ship as it bucked and tossed through the waves.

The next surge crossed the boat from the other side, and the sailors screamed and scrabbled to hang on as the water rushed across the deck. Ilmatar felt that the sea was making a mockery of the boat, for even though it floated through the water, it did nothing to prevent the ocean from covering the sailors. Only the pauses between the waves gave them time to breathe and prepare for the next assault.

Ilmatar began to wonder if any of them would even make it to Tuonela alive.

As the ship crossed over a high wave and pounded down the trough to the next wave, Ilmatar noticed glowing green seaweed all around the boat.

Then she noticed the seaweed was moving by itself, and hope swelled inside her with renewed power.

She watched all around her, lunging across the boat along with the thrust of the wave, to the other side. She managed to reach the wheel by holding onto the ropes along the side rails, and looking astern she saw nothing but green seaweed as far as she could look.

Two sailors were thrown overboard, and they fell to the sea, their screams tugged away by the vicious winds. At that moment, several of the seaweed clusters disappeared, and bodies rose out of the water, each bearing six arms.

The many-armed Nakki spun their appendages through the air, and pushed the sailors back up onto the deck.

Cato and Alzena watched in amazement as the green-tinted transparent faces smiled back at them, clear water pulsing through their veins instead of blood. Their eyes were as blue as the depths of the ocean.

Ilmatar was standing close to Cato and Alzena, and as the storm paused for a second to gather more strength, she turned to them. "Those are the Nakki. They live to save the lives of drowning men and women."

As she stared at this massive seaweed collection, blond hair began flowing out of the water, and below them, fresh faces emerged from the depths.

The mermaids swam in a circle around the boat.

In unison, the mermaids rolled to their backs, one by one, and each one presented six arms to the sky, spinning them in a circle as if they were dancing.

Then, combined with this powerful dance, the Nakki began to sing, all at once, a most beautiful song.

She heard hundreds and hundreds of Nakki singing in perfect harmony with each other, so each part sounded like one voice, but in a perfect three-part harmony; they were deafening. Ilmatar knew the Nakki had powerful magic.

By the last time they raised their voices, Ukko had traveled across the nebula to reach her. She felt relief wash over her as the haunting melody stirred her soul.

"*Thy founder was the Lord of Hosts,*
Who made the earth and swelling sea:
And while their strong foundations stand,
Thy name men's wonder shall command."

Over and over again they sang, increasing the power and the pitch of the melody until the clouds began to drift away and the waves began to settle into smooth swells.

The night sky grew clear and the stars twinkled overhead, while the light of the two moons turned the northern sky into a glowing yellow bowl for the moons to float in.

The sailors worked on mopping the water off the deck and wringing out the sails as life returned to normal on the *Urwind*. The Nakki disappeared into the night, thinking all was well. Ilmatar had not revealed to them the ship was headed for Tuonela. Had they known, they would have done everything in their power to convince them to turn around.

Ilmatar thought about the Nakki as they sailed away, and reminded herself that she was willing to do whatever she had to do for her small child.

Even though she had never been able to hold the child, she knew what it was like to hold a baby, and now the feeling of emptiness between her arms was becoming a crushing vacuum as her human emotions began to wash over her in waves.

The feelings inside her were stronger than the ones she dealt with as a goddess, and she was unprepared for their ferocity.

Overwhelming grief crowded in on her, pushing her arms together against her will, until she found herself praying, bending, becoming fully human.

Realizing that she was becoming vulnerable, Ilmatar shuddered, pulling herself together. She walked to her cabin so she would not be seen.

Chapter Nineteen

As they sailed across the open ocean, Cato kept one hand on the wheel, gazing out to sea. From time to time, Alzena would check her map against her brass sextant to ensure they were headed the right way. Each time she would tell Cato, "Keep going."

Ilmatar lost all sense of time and space as they crossed the trackless sea. Things that once occupied her knowledge as a goddess began to lose their meaning on this endless swath of water, white on the sunward side and deep blue on the skyward side.

She had no idea how long they had been traveling, but when she gathered her wits, night had already fallen and she realized she was the only one on deck except for Cato, who tirelessly held fast to the wheel. She forced herself to her feet and went to her cabin to rest, feeling the need for sleep, and spent the night peacefully in her hammock.

Cato arose the next morning to find a strange sight, a dark cloud gathering above him. He pointed up, and some of the sailors looked up in alarm as well.

Everyone on board witnessed a great dark cloud swirl in the sky above the ship. General alarm sprung up on board.

Cato stared into the deepening pool of dark clouds above his head.

"This wouldn't have anything to do with your stormy brother Ukko, would it?"

Ilmatar stared defiantly at Cato. "That's not Ukko's type of storm. Something really bad is happening. That's the same color as the clouds that blew overhead when my child was stolen!"

"Everyone alert!" cried Cato. "Get all the hands on deck! We need every weapon we have to win today!"

Alzena ducked behind some boxes on deck and quickly made her way to Cato. Ilmatar ducked as well.

"Cato! I know how to stop them. They're Surmas! Don't let the talons touch your sailors. You have to aim below their neck and fire with lightning speed! Avoid their talons, men!"

As the men scrambled for their bows and spears, dozens of screeching creatures flew from the storm cloud and descended towards the boat in sweeping circles. Some of the faster Surmas had already shot past the sail, cutting two sailors with their talons when they tried to fight them off. Hot blood spurted from their arms, and as the poison took hold, they screamed in pain.

"Watch yourselves!" cried Cato. "These creatures don't fight fair!"

The cuts quickly boiled and widened, and the sailors cried out. Cato knew he had to do something fast. Dozens more Surmas began to descend in all directions, and Cato felt a new sense of urgency.

He knelt down before the weapon and prayed fervently.

"Goddess of Light, please hear my prayer in this moment of need! I need arrows fast enough to embrace the speed of light. Let my arrows pierce so fast the darkness inside these Surmas' souls rips their condemned bodies to shreds!"

As huge piles of arrows and bows appeared before him out of thin air, Cato began handing them out to the unharmed sailors as quickly as he could. Arming himself as well, he aimed his bow to the sky. "Fire as quickly as possible! Speed is of the essence!"

Volleys of arrows plunged into the sky faster than Ilmatar could track them. With neck-breaking speed, they plunged into their targets, yanking them backward.

As the Surma above Cato plunged backward, his neck snapped forward so violently the sailors could hear the crunch over the screams of the other Surmas as they drew closer. The arrows were not fast enough to stop all of the Surmas, and some flew past the sails as well, cutting into the sailors with their talons.

The sailors continued to fight with vigor, and Cato picked off the Surmas with lightning speed. Ilmatar had trouble watching his arm as it flung arrow after arrow. It was like a blur.

Chapter Twenty

Tursas was growing restless as his plans slowly eroded. He had wanted hundreds of souls, especially Cato's. Cato still had a great deal of power, even though his curse had been lifted years ago.

He paced in front of Milla and Andri's prisons. He glared at them through the bars. Although he had reduced them to prisoners, the ancient god and goddess continued to stare back at him defiantly. No matter how hard he tried to destroy their spirits, they remained defiant, not letting their faith leave them.

As he had been doing for centuries, Tursas continued to torture them.

"I'm so sick and tired of your pathetic realm. When I took over, I thought I was getting something good! Power! Souls! Dominion!" He continued to pace back and forth. "But this is what I get? A rotten, desolate, boring world full of dead creatures! What kind of kingdom is this? I'll tell you what kind of kingdom this is! It's just like you—pathetic and weak!" He stopped pacing and advanced on the cage, staring Milla right in the face. "But I've got big plans. When I take over the world of the living, oh, then we'll see some action around here! With the world of the living under my control, I can bend these miserable people to my will. I have plans for these people, many kingdoms for them to occupy. If you behave, I might even let you rule one of them."

Tursas walked away from the cages. Then he stopped and turned around slowly. "No, you know what? I think I'd rather keep you right here as my pets! You don't even deserve to leave these cages."

As Tursas turned around again and departed, disappearing down the long stone staircases, Milla and Andri continued to hold hands, staring at each other and smiling. Although Tursas was twisted, he had overlooked the fact that they could now hold hands, and having that ability, they could have hope.

Now that hope had been renewed, they knew Tursas would someday be destroyed. They no longer cared what he shouted and threatened in his vain attempts to torture them.

Tursas returned to where the dragon was chained in a deep part of the cavern. The dragon traveled back and forth through the pit, as far as his chain would allow, turning and roaring ferociously when it noticed Tursas standing at the edge of the pit.

"I'm disappointed in you, dragon! You failed miserably in Santara. You only claimed eighteen souls. Eighteen! And you didn't even manage to kill Cato!"

The dragon's black heart pounded under Tursas's spell. The dragon panted for breath, crying out in pain and bending toward the floor. It pushed itself back with its strong legs. Gaining ground, it raised its head and growled menacingly at Tursas.

"The one you put inside me was struggling with me!" complained the dragon. "It tried to distract me. And the Lion-People put big holes in my wings with their rocks. I fought them all at the castle, but they made me retreat before I could claim any souls at all. Then I attacked them by the village, but a powerful spear drove me back!"

Loviatar began to awaken deep inside the dragon. She could tell how badly the dragon was damaged and began to heal its wings and the injury from the spear. She left his twisted mind alone, pressing instead to heal his body. A blue glow began to surround the dragon.

Tursas saw immediately, and noticed with rage that the tears in the wing skin were being healed. He knew that, given enough power, the goddess inside of him could heal his mind, and he would be able to turn against Tursas.

Tursas vowed he would never let that happen. With his dark magic, he twisted the dragon even further, pushing Loviatar's awareness into submission and twisting more ropes of hatred around her, trapping her deep inside the dragon's heart.

The blue glow faded to a translucent shimmer and Tursas knew her power had been weakened. He stopped before he killed the goddess, because without her, the dragon's heart would be left without power and he would return to the dead, buried in the useless rocks.

The powerful wings hung limp at each side, powerless in agony. Without even touching the dragon, Tursas moved his hands from side to side, and the wings moved against the dragon's will, bent by Tursas's force. The dragon knew Tursas had complete control over it and bowed its head deeply, pressing it against the ground.

"Mercy!" roared the dragon. "Mercy!"

The pressure halted, and the dragon stared up at Tursas, this time with terror and submission. Panting, it lowered its head again, this time all the way to stone floor below.

"I have stopped punishing you for one reason only. I will give you another chance to prove yourself."

The dragon looked up, paying close attention.

"I need you to travel to the land beyond Farralina, beyond a mountain range and finally a wide ocean, called the Land of the Musaat. You will know it by its powerful city with seven towers. Give me as many souls as you can gather. You failed last time! Don't fail me again! I need the power of the Musaat! Break through and capture them so I can use their powers to capture and spell every living being. Then I will be the only god that means anything to them, and the other gods will finally be destroyed!"

Tursas swiped his hands dismissively and the shackles binding the black dragon separated at his will. Tursas once again opened his hands wide, and a crack began to form in the roof of the cavern, widening and glowing red as it separated. The open space between the edges of the rift turned clear and free. The rift expanded until the world of the living could be easily reached.

The dragon flapped its giant wings and ascended to the air, flying slowly out of the cavern, along with many Surmas flying in tandem.

After the dragon and the Surmas had departed, Tursas pushed his hands back together, and the rift slowly closed above him. With a hissing and finally a great crunch, the rocks sealed back together.

Then Tursas fell to the stone, clutching at it with his fingertips, panting for breath. He curled up in a ball, his legs shaking, his brain catching fire with burning pain. Every time Tursas altered reality, it took a terrible toll on his body, one he was very careful to hide from the Surmas by sending them on the mission as well.

As the pain began to go away, Tursas rose to his feet again and grabbed a vial of potion from a hiding place deep inside his robe. From the vial, Tursas drank some of his ethereal potion, one he had stolen from a goddess named Kide centuries ago. The potion kept him vibrant and alive, even here in the Land of the Dead. After drinking the potion, Tursas rested.

Chapter Twenty-One

The black dragon exited the portal and passed above the fog, flying so high in the air he could see almost all of Santara. The Surmas caught up with him and hovered nearby, waiting for his urge.

The ocean lay between them and their destination, and mountains and fields and forests, but the dragon had a mission. He urged the Surmas onward, to the Land of the Muses.

A deep ocean separated the Land of the Muses from the rest of the continents on Santara. The dragon could see the massive city from far above, and at his cry, the Surmas swooped down, matching his fall as they tumbled towards the city, relentless.

Although Malkin and the other musicians did quite well, and the dancers performed as well as they could, the audience began to grow bored. Calliope, the Musaat of Music, could tell the performers were off their game from where she looked down from the tower.

She descended slowly, knowing full well it was forbidden to leave. She wanted to inspire the performers.

As the black dragon continued to plummet, Calliope was in the audience, inspiring the dancers and the musicians on stage. She had decided not to use her invisibility cloak, never a good thing for the Musaat. In this one way, the Musaat were allowed to leave their towers and meet travelers in public, but they were forbidden to be in sight even then, remaining cloaked.

Calliope sent waves of magic to the performers, and the bright colors twinkled through the air, surrounding them. They began to dance swooping forms, sweeping around the stage, while the music became a symphony, echoing through the audience. People in the audience began to dance back and forth, caught up in the moment. Only Calliope saw what was happening as the dragon plummeted toward the city.

"Dragon!" Calliope screamed at the top of her lungs.

Malkin reacted to her cry by lunging away from the stage. He got away at the same time that the dragon crashed into the roof, avoiding certain death by mere seconds. He sent a prayer of gratitude to Calliope for rescuing him, but realized that everyone else on stage was already dead.

Seven performers were singing and dancing on one of the three Great Stages when the dragon plummeted, crashing into the roof hard enough to destroy the columns beneath and send it crashing to the stage.

The dragon watched twelve souls rise up through the roof and merge with his body as he consumed them, preserving them for the wizard. Those that were not destroyed were dragged away by the Surmas to present to Tursas for his control. They were destined to become Surmas as well, helpless servants for as long as Tursas reigned.

Malkin squared his shoulders and prepared for battle. He had no intention of fleeing in a time of crisis.

Many people ran for their lives as Surmas landed in the city and started fighting the locals.

Another Musaat, Euterpe, came down from her own tower. Cloaked with invisibility, Euterpe brought down three of the Surmas with her powerful magic.

The dragon was horrified at the possibility of another punishment from the dreaded Tursas, and quickly started delivering commands to the confused Surmas. "Get that one, right there! The one you can still see! She would make an excellent prize! Leave the other one alone! She'll just keep on destroying you. You're no use to me dead."

The Surmas stopped trying to attack the invisible Musaat and concentrated their forces on the one that was out in the open, still defeating Surmas on her own, but infinitely more vulnerable.

Calliope knew she was in trouble when the Surmas began to surround her. But a bloodcurdling scream erupted from behind the creatures. Malkin jumped forward, tearing the throat of one of the Surmas, which drew the attention of the other two, while others arrived to join in the fray.

"I'll protect you," cried Malkin, shielding her with his massive arms.

Malkin struck another Surma against the neck, and it stopped moving. Calliope gasped, feeling her strength drain away. Being touched by a mortal, she was losing her power, and without her power, she couldn't escape back to her tower where she would be safe. Malkin, while trying to protect her, was actually making her more vulnerable.

The soldiers came near, fighting to protect Calliope as well. Malkin relished the support and quickly assisted soldiers and other fighters in stopping the winged beasts.

The science building not too far behind them began to collapse, while Surmas continued to destroy the foundation, eager to bring the entire structure to ruin.

The dragon sensed Malkin's strength, and wrapped his long tail around him. The spikes gored the lion man, although his thick fur protected him slightly. He roared in pain and stopped trying to fight.

The dragon lifted his tail into the air, unrolling it, and dropped Malkin to the ground. He fell and did not try to get back up. The townspeople surrounded the fallen man.

"Let's get him into the mathematics building," one of them cried. "It's the strongest building in the city!"

After overwhelming her, the Surmas pulled Calliope from the ground, and flew away with her back to Tuonela.

Calliope could see the portal and the underworld, but couldn't fight against the strength of a dragon. As she passed over, she felt extremely weakened and remembered that her powers had no strength in Tuonela. She screamed when she saw the evil wizard, but he leered right back.

"Congratulations, black dragon! This is an excellent prize. You will be rewarded this time." Tursas bobbed up and down with excitement.

"You'll never stop us!" Calliope shouted, fighting against her captors.

"Get her tied down!" commanded the wizard.

The Musaat writhed when she saw the place she was destined for. Surrounded by darkness and tied to dark forces, the stones the Surmas were tying her to were covered in blood.

"How many souls did you get for me this time?" he asked.

"Hundreds," growled the dragon, completely in the wizard's thrall.

"Well, give them to me then!" said Tursas. "I need to complete the spell!"

The dragon opened his mouth and essences of hundreds of souls poured forth. Tursas spread his arms above his head and blue smoke curled around his hands, drawing the pale souls to his grasp. Inside his hands, they coalesced and flowed. He left several clutched inside his hands for another, much darker, purpose.

Calliope trembled as Tursas drew closer. Her divine skin shone in the light, even in the evil orange glow of Tuonela. Her face, ordinarily a smiling source of inspiration and hope, was now a mask of terror.

Tursas stared at the Musaat. "You understand, don't you? I need you to help me complete my journey."

The Musaat refused to open her mouth, even to scream, though her eyes said it all.

"Get her mouth open!" screamed Tursas. "I'm going to turn her whether she likes it or not!"

A nearby Surma took the advantage and forced her mouth wide open. The Musaat struggled and forced it closed again, but the Surma mauled her ear and she couldn't help but scream.

Tursas pushed the communion of souls up against Calliope's lips. As her scream went out, the souls went in, pulling themselves down her throat and bending her will. Calliope choked and gagged as the slippery soul-matter slipped like grease past her lips and down her throat, and she felt a transformation begin as her insides twisted and bulged, becoming something new and hideous.

Tursas knew this was no ordinary creature in his grasp. This was a supreme creature, a daughter of the gods, and something he could use to his own gain.

The Musaat transformed before his eyes, black hair turning to gray, and her deep brown eyes turned a sick, glowing yellow, staring at Tursas with pure malice. The shining skin went from fair to rugged and pockmarked.

Tursas spoke to his new creation. "You were once a servant of the divine. Now you have a new purpose. Henceforth you shall serve only me, your new Lord and Master, Tursas!"

The creature bowed down before Tursas as far as her restraints would allow.

"What would you command me to do, Lord Tursas?"

Tursas smiled broadly at the title, but did not take his gaze away. "I need you to capture all of your Musaat sisters. Bring them to me!"

Tursas wielded his magic and the chains were broken. As the creature that was once Calliope stepped forward, she discovered two wings behind her back, and she took flight for the Land of the Musaat.

Chapter Twenty-Two

Alzena stayed protected behind the barrels on the deck of the *Ur-wind*, lopping wings off left and right. She stood up and looked across the deck. Many Surmas had fallen, but were still twitching their wings. Moans and shudders filled the air. Alzena knew they were done for, but decided to put them out their misery.

A protective maternal instinct came over her as she heard the suffering sailors and her blood ran hot with rage.

Alzena pulled the sharp dagger from her belt and walked up to the nearest Surma, still flapping its useless wings. She raised the dagger high above her head so the ruby glinted in the sun. The Surma stared up at her as she dealt the killing blow, but as it died, its eyes closed forever.

She went along to the next one, burying the dagger into its neck again, and this time, the Surma died much faster.

As she continued to stab the Surmas, the wind swept across the deck, and the sunlight began to beam down on their bodies, turning them to dust and ash before her eyes and sweeping them off into the waves. Alzena stood up, knowing her job was done, and realized the cries were coming from the sailors now.

All around the ship, men lay upon the deck, with cuts that grew deeper as the poison worked its way in. They moaned in agony, and Alzena realized she needed Ilmatar's help.

"Where are you, Ilmatar?"

Ilmatar ran down to the main deck. "Get these men inside. Where's the cook?"

"Right here."

Ilmatar looked around but couldn't see him. Then he began to stand up from behind the crates.

"What are you doing down there?" asked Ilmatar.

"I'm the most important man on the ship! Except for you, Your Majesty," he added nervously to Cato. He appeared flustered. "Without me, everyone on board would go hungry."

Alzena shot him an insulted glare.

"I'm headed down to the kitchen to get all the medicine I can find," said Ilmatar. "I might have my potions, but I think I'll need a little more than that today."

"Right away," said the astonished cook and bustled down to the mess hall and the kitchen while Ilmatar fetched her potions in their small bottles.

The kitchen was a mess after the interrupted morning meal, but the cook had managed to preserve the medicine. She quickly poured Pau d'Arco, goldenseal, and other choice medicines into a pan of water. Then she started pouring the blue potion into the pan as well. The cook stared in amazement.

"Where in the world did you get these potions from?"

"From the nebula around this planet. I come from the stars. I'm a goddess. Didn't they tell you that?"

"Well, you know, there's rumors, but I don't like to listen to gossip." His face turned red again and he stopped talking. Ilmatar stirred the brewing potion in silence, smiling faintly.

When the potion was complete, Ilmatar poured it into a bowl and started into the back of the ship, where the injured sailors were waiting.

When she got there, the cook looked at her inquiringly.

"I need your help," said Ilmatar. "Find me strips of sailcloth, lots and lots of them. I need to bind the paste against their wounds to heal them."

The cook was more useful than she thought, because within seconds she heard many ripping sounds, and before long at all she was presented with a decent-sized pile of scraps.

"That will be perfect for binding," she said. "Let's get started."

Ilmatar knelt in front of the first injured sailor as he lay in the cabin. He was a fighter, brave and determined to survive, though some of his fellow sailors were already lying silent on the floor.

Ilmatar covered his arm in paste where the cut was deepest. The paste quickly removed the poison, and the potion she'd infused helped knit the muscle back together. As the man's arm slowly began to heal, the cook wrapped the wound in gauze to keep it safe. She moved on to the next man.

He was on his back, silent, and she thought for sure he was destined for the watery grave. But his eyes snapped open when she put the paste on his chest, and even though he sputtered and used foul language, he eventually quieted down as his ribs began to knit and his lungs began to regain their proper function. The blue went out of his lips as he recovered, and he smiled weakly at Ilmatar.

"Rest easy now, the cook will bind you up."

As she moved on to the third man, she realized he had already passed on and there was nothing her potion could do for him. She closed his eyes very slowly, and silently moved on to the next man, while the cook avoided the dead man completely.

Chapter Twenty-Three

After the harrowing battle and the chaos of the morning, everyone on board was feasting mightily. The long wooden tables were decked in meat and preserved fruits, and there was a general air of merriment. Even Cato and Alzena were in their finest clothing, and the drinks were flowing freely.

Ilmatar didn't touch her drink, or her food, but simply stared out into the distance as if something was bothering her. When the sailor burst in from the deck, Ilmatar was the only one who noticed.

The sailor quickly approached Cato's side with a scrap of paper.

Cato looked at it and hung his head in his hands.

Alzena looked over at Cato. "Cato! What's wrong?"

"He's attacked again, Alzena. This time he burned the Land of the Musaat. He captured one of the Musaat and he even killed those people that danced at our wedding! We have to do something!"

The goddess Uta appeared before Cato, intervening. "Wait! You don't know the whole story! My children are safe, I promise you. The gods miss nothing; fear not, for you shall prevail!"

Cato paused in his action. "On second thought, we are very close to the dragon itself. We should press on while we have the advantage. As long as he keeps foraging on more attacks, the more his resources will be spread thin, and the easier it will be to take the advantage. What do you think, Alzena?"

Alzena answered carefully. "We are almost to our destination. We can't let ourselves get distracted. Others will take care of them."

His people nodded, and Ilmatar nodded as well, although she had seen Uta intervene. Unlike the sailors, Ilmatar had enough of a goddess left in her to witness the other spirits at work.

"So we continue to our destination," said Cato. "But first let us pray for those who have fallen."

As the sailors prayed, Ilmatar slid one of the knives from the table into the folds of her dress and quietly arose to leave the table. She wondered if any one of the sailors even remembered that, mere hours ago, she had been saving their hides from certain death.

Even if they remembered her healing potion, they continued to pray with their heads lowered as she exited the mess hall entirely. She continued on her mission, finding her quarters completely empty, like every berth on the ship. Everyone but her was in the mess hall.

At first she was happy to be alone. Before long, though, she began to realize that nobody else was guarding the ship. None of them were manning the sails. She suddenly felt extremely vulnerable. She realized the time to cast the spell was now, when no one could observe her.

Silently, she began to prepare.

Chapter Twenty-Four

Deep inside the ship, Ilmatar sat within her cabin, preparing for a ritual that would let her see her young baby, desperate to glimpse her beautiful face. She watched the simmering red potion fill the bowl, splashing back and forth as it filled.

Ilmatar raised the knife from its hiding place and dragged the sharp edge along her hand, drawing a line of blood from her mortal body. The sensation of pain was different this time, hot and burning, and she winced as the red blood began to drip from her veins.

She felt faint as it spilled into the bowl. She knew she had enough blood, and quickly wrapped her hand in a rag to stop the bleeding before she got too weak.

Breathing deeply so she wouldn't lose consciousness, Ilmatar raised the bowl from its place on the table and placed it over the small fire she had carefully built in a clay bowl. Surrounding the bowl, she had packed bundles of soaking wet bamboo she had found in the hold. She wanted to make sure the fire didn't spread to the wooden hull of the ship by any means.

The vapors rose, red and menacing, into the air, disguising the fire smoke in a blood-red haze that began to fill the room.

A normal mortal would have been terrified out of his mind by the quickly maturing spell, but Ilmatar was not afraid of such things.

She generously sucked in the vapor, expecting her daughter's divine face to appear any second now before her. The spell should have been instantaneous, but even after several inhalations, she still failed to see any visions. She began to wonder if she had managed to botch the spell somehow when a terrific ringing began in her ears. With a jolt, she realized the spell was starting to work.

As she stared into the bowl, a horrific apparition appeared before her. A face materialized in the bowl, but it was not her daughter's face. It was a hideous dragon, blackened and twisted. Evil red eyes stared back at her, horribly aware. Two words escaped the dragon's blood-drenched fangs. "Hello, Mother."

Ilmatar fell to her knees. A tremendous pain shot out from her chest, and hot tears began to flow. All these feelings were new to her, and she tried to cope with each wave of pain.

She dumped the bowl into the fire, splashing the magical contents, causing it to explode into a tower of flame before being extinguished. Ilmatar surveyed the ceiling, dousing any sparks that lingered with a cup of water. Then she leaned back, shock overwhelming her. It felt like her heart was being ripped out of her chest with horror. Human tears, hot and salty, began to flow down her face, and she dropped to the floor with the realization that her daughter was now the dreaded black dragon, the same creature they had come to Tuonela to destroy.

Hours later, Ilmatar stood on the deck with Alzena, looking out to sea.

"You've been very quiet during dinner, and now you've been out here all night. People are looking for you," said Alzena.

"I had to know for sure, Alzena. What had become of my daughter." With her hands shaking, Ilmatar said, "I looked deep inside the magic and discovered a black dragon staring back at me."

Alzena looked at Ilmatar with horror. "What are you saying?" she asked.

"I'm afraid if you break the curse, you'll kill my daughter in the process!" Ilmatar broke down in sobs, and the startled Alzena could only reach out to comfort her.

Alzena whispered to Ilmatar. "I promise that Cato and I will find a way to save Loviatar. We came all this way to rescue her, and that's what we intend to do."

Ilmatar hugged Alzena, mostly to hide the surprise in her eyes. "There has to be a way," she cried. "I can't lose her."

"I brought many of the scrolls along with me on the ship. We'll stay up all night looking through them if we have to. We'll find a way."

In the biggest sleeping quarters on the ship, Queen Alzena and Ilmatar pored through the scrolls and books, searching for more information about the Land of the Dead, and everything they could find out about Tursas's curse. They read by yellow lamplight, looking for some clue they might have missed.

Alzena cried out, "I found something!"

Ilmatar went over to where Alzena was reading a massive manuscript. She had her finger marking the page while the magnificent cover was closed. An emblazoned image of a swan decorated the front with ornate designs surrounding it and appearing to melt the swan into the book.

Around each corner the book was reinforced with brass pieces, and strips of bronze and copper were hammered into the spine, reinforcing the leather strips that held the book together.

Although Alzena loved to keep surprises, she couldn't hide the way she shook her hand when her finger was free of the book. She held the lantern directly overhead so Ilmatar could see the brilliantly colored paintings inside.

The paintings did more justice to Tuonela than the words of the historians. She saw pictures of dead trees, lost souls, burning lava, rocks that she thought were red but other pictures revealed to be blood, and worst of all, a black river pouring through a cavern with no light at the end. All these pictures surrounded the words, bringing the stories to life. Ilmatar stared in horror at this dead world her baby was living in.

"What do they call this horrible river?" Ilmatar asked.

"It says this river is called Tuonelan Virta, or the River of the Dead." Alzena shuddered.

"What a horrible place we're going," said Ilmatar. "I don't even know how the Surmas can survive down there."

"It talks here about the blood summoning the Great Dragon. This happened a very long time ago, during the reign of King Hartti."

"Who was King Hartti?" asked Ilmatar.

"He was my great-great-great grandfather, but he was not a very great king at all. The family never said much about him. Even the history books had his name erased. I'm surprised his name even remained in this book! Somebody must have hidden it during the purge, when they erased his existence from every record they could find. That was hundreds of years ago. Whoever hid this book is long gone by now."

"What does it say about the dragon? Keep going!"

"Hartti prayed to Tursas, because he was a greedy king. Tursas promised Hartti what he wanted—dozens of kingdoms to himself. Tursas warned him that he wanted his soul once he died. Hartti agreed anyway, and gave up his soul for his future. But before he could claim the kingdoms, Tursas betrayed him, and he ended up dying on the battlefield before even conquering his first kingdom. His people were overpowered. Tursas never sent the reinforcements he promised. As he died, Tursas stole his soul, which was powerful enough to revive the Great Dragon, a mighty creature that had been dead for centuries."

"Does it say anything else about this black dragon?"

Alzena read further. "Tursas used his powerful blood as part of the spell, but other blood was involved too. He always has to use the blood of a god or goddess. In that long-ago time, it was the blood of the God Ahto, who Tursas had destroyed."

"Does that mean my daughter is still alive inside the dragon?"

"Yes, Loviatar is still alive, or the dragon would have returned to the dead. This scroll says the goddess has to stay alive to feed her life to the dragon. The dragons are lifeless without the power of the gods."

"But won't Loviatar be harmed?"

"Only the dragon will be wounded, not the goddess inside. Loviatar has been sent to another plane of existence and won't be touched. There's a special spear called The Bane of the Dragons buried in the Graveyard of the Dragons. If you obtain this weapon, you will only kill the dragon, releasing its twisted spirit, but leaving the goddess intact. I'm sure she will be very weak, though. We will have to get her out of there as fast as possible."

"That means we have to deal with Tursas at the same time," said Ilmatar.

"If he sends the dragons to attack us, Cato and I will do everything we can to keep your daughter safe. I promise you as a mother."

Alzena looked deeply into Ilmatar's eyes, recognizing the deep fire that burned inside every mother when their baby was threatened.

"Come," said Alzena. "We must rest, for tomorrow we should be arriving at the portal to Tuonela."

Chapter Twenty-Five

Ilmatar stood on deck the next morning and watched as an orange-red fog began to billow above the waters. As the mists thickened around the boat, Alzena came up behind her.

"We're getting close now," she said. "All that you see before you is the barrier that divides the Land of the Dead from the rest of the world." Alzena turned to Cato. "Don't turn the wheel, no matter what you do. Go straight through the fog and you'll emerge on the other side. Turn, and I guarantee you'll be lost forever."

Cato kept his hand firm on the wheel, refusing to turn. For hours, they drifted through the fog, with barely a breeze to keep them going. The fog grew thicker and thicker around them until it became dark. Cato couldn't even see his hand on the wheel, and relied on muscular willpower to keep his hand steady. It became a game of patience, and the deathly silence perpetrated by the suffocating fog drove him mad until he heard singing and voices interrupt the silence. It was all he could do to keep his hand steady.

"Help!"

Cato knew the voices were tempting him.

"We're drowning!"

He felt an instinct to turn the boat and save the sailors, but he knew he was hallucinating and refused to deviate from his course.

As the hallucinations continued, Cato discovered it took more and more willpower to ignore them.

"Save us!" cried the voices.

"Don't abandon us!" others begged.

Cato was being peppered with doubt, convinced the fog would never lift, when he realized he could see his hand again, and not long after that, the wheel he was still gripping. He noticed patches of light shining through the fog bank, and before he knew it, they had broken free, and the sailors cheered at the clear sky that shone above them. He noticed that all his sailors were still on the boat, and was relieved to see that every single voice had indeed been a cruel temptation.

"Keep alert, men! We're not out of the woods yet! We're about to enter the Land of the Dead. Keep your wits about you and you'll come back out alive. Lose your mind now, and you're never returning from Tuonela. I'll try to keep you all alive, but we are traveling into great danger. I wouldn't have brought you here if I didn't think you could handle it."

Although Cato had his doubts, the sailors turned as one to face the portal and gazed at their destination without a single unsteady leg on deck.

A huge shimmering blue portal shone before them, floating on the ocean in a half-circle. Beyond the half-circle, Ilmatar could see a paradise of green tropical trees, sweeping beaches, and hills covered in vegetation.

"What a beautiful place this is!" said Alzena. "This must be the most beautiful place in all of Santara! Why would this be called the Land of the Dead?"

"This is merely an illusion to draw in hapless travelers. You will see, once we enter, that the Land of the Dead is not a fit place for any creature, living or dead," Ilmatar replied.

Alzena felt nauseated when they reached the portal. Skeletons reached through the portal, screaming, and popped back into the blue light. The rift didn't open seamlessly, but tore in sections.

Traveling through the dangerous zone, Ilmatar felt so dizzy she had to sit down, and noticed some of the sailors falling to their knees, as well. It was like she was being put to sleep. She felt so extremely tired. One by one, every single one of them fell asleep.

When they woke up, they discovered they were sailing down a black river, and the world of the living was far behind them.

A deep cavern surrounded them, beneath which a black river flowed, carrying them further into the cavern and into Tuonela. Orange hues clung to the walls, and fires crackled in odd places in the cavern walls. Strange shrieks from distant places echoed quietly as they sailed onward.

Rounding a bend in the river, Alzena looked up from her scroll, where the Graveyard of the Dragons was marked, and noticed the walls and a wide iron gate that marked a graveyard.

"Maybe that's the graveyard you're looking for," she said.

"Drop the anchor," cried Cato. The heavy chain clanged wildly as the anchor plummeted through the dark water of the Tuonelan Virta.

The boat came to a halt and the dinghy was lowered into the black water. Cato and a few sailors descended the rope ladder to the small boat below.

"Let's see what's in this strange world out there," said Cato.

The men were clearly growing uneasy, but something inside of them stirred when Cato spoke. They moved as one, silent. In unison, the oars hit the black water, and it splashed over the white oar blades and stained them a sickening gray, growing darker with each stroke.

The water was thicker than seawater, clinging to the oars as they parted the murky depths, and Cato dared not stick his hand into it. The boat reached a shallow shoreline, and ran aground smoothly. Cato and the sailors hopped off the end of the dinghy to the shore, careful not to touch the water.

"We need to learn more about this place. Find anything you can."

Cato and the sailors crossed the beach, approaching the gate of the graveyard.

"This doesn't look quite right," said Cato. "I don't see any dragon skulls."

He turned around slowly, studying the cavern more closely. A surge of movement in the sand caught his attention as he was scanning, and he paused.

"The sand just moved," said Cato.

"Nonsense," said one of the sailors. "Sand can't move on its own."

"It can in the Land of the Dead."

Cato drew his sword to distract the slug rearing up behind the sailor. The slug was covered in sand, although it fell away from its slimy skin in a steady rain.

"Sand slugs!" cried Cato. "Don't waste your lives on these useless creatures. Run!"

The sailor ducked and screamed, rolling out of the way as Cato started to battle the slug. The Sword of Light was not much use unless he was up against the worst kind of creatures. Fortunately for Cato, the sand worms were very evil, like the evil spirits that had spawned these monsters so long ago, so the sword did considerable damage, shearing it in two and leaving the slug divided and twitching, spewing sand with every kick.

"I think it's time to get back to the boat!" yelled Cato. "We're in the wrong place!"

As the sailors ran for the safety of the dinghy, the slugs chased them down the beach, slithering across the sand. Cato kept them at bay with the Sword of Light until the sailors all reached the dinghy. As Cato leaped in behind them, he unbalanced the dinghy and had to control the rocking by pumping his legs back and forth. When Cato was steady, the sailors started rowing away.

The sand slugs chased after them, but they stopped by the black water of the Tuonelan Virta and refused to touch the foul-colored liquid at all, letting Cato and the sailors escape on the dinghy.

Chapter Twenty-Six

Cato and the *Urwind* traveled down the black river until they reached a massive graveyard. Two dragon skulls were half-buried in the sand by the shore.

Cato turned to Alzena. "Two dragon heads! Now that's more like it!"

Alzena nodded. "I think this is definitely the place for sure. No sand slugs running amuck on the beach either. This is much better."

"This is where the weapon lies buried!" said Cato. "Now it's safe to disembark."

Alzena followed close behind. "That depends on what you mean by safe. Last time you barely made it back to the boat. I'm helping you this time."

Cato paused and extended his arm. "After you, my queen."

They returned to the dinghy and slowly rowed to shore. The sailors grew unsettled by the size of the skulls and looked at each other nervously.

A pair of rocks narrowed the channel to a close range. Passing this obstacle, Cato had an unobstructed view of the beach. Skeletons lay above ground, human and beast alike, scattered across the shore. The bones were independent of each other, and Cato realized that even the dead had no peace in Tuonela. The sand on the beach was probably powdered bone by the time he got to shore and he felt the unnatural crunch beneath his feet again.

Dragon skulls lay at odd angles, massive jawbones jutting toward a cavern roof. The top of the jawbone was higher in the air than a villager's home, but even though they could easily pass beneath it, none of the sailors felt compelled to travel under those massive teeth, even if the flesh had rotted away thousands of years ago. Instead, they walked around them, even though the troubled bones continued to inch closer.

Cato and the sailors treaded carefully, although it was apparent even the slugs avoided this hostile place.

Alzena said, "I remember Valo saying that only the Sword of Light can shine on the grave. No other light will shine upon it."

Cato raised the sword high above his head. "Show me the Bane of the Dragons! Shine your light upon this weapon." Though there was no light in the cavern, save for the sickening orange glow from fires burning deep inside, the Sword of Light shone with an unearthly yellow light throughout the musty cavern. The beam shot out and shone across a bridge and upon a rock face beyond.

The bridge was made from dragon bones tied together with strips of ancient hide, and looked very unstable.

The people crossing the bridge ahead of Alzena must have weakened it; the bones beneath Alzena's feet gave way as the ancient hide tore with a strange ripping sound.

Alzena fell through the torn bridge, grabbing a bone with both hands and screaming, "I'm not dying down here! Cato!"

Cato heard his wife's cry and threw himself down on his stomach, grabbing her hands tightly and raising her back up from the abyss as more dragon bones fell behind her.

They made it across the rest of the bridge, but soon fell upon another problem. Where the sand mixed with the water flowing down to the Tuonelan Virta from the world above, quicksand lurked unseen beneath their feet. Two of his sailors nearby began sinking. He reached out a hand to each one to keep them steady, but a third man sank further. Cato roared in pain but could do nothing as the third man sank to his doom. The quicksand continued to suck at the two sailors he grasped, and pulling them out took a great deal of strength and time. While they were being extracted, the small movements of the third sailor beneath the sand finally stopped. After Cato pulled the sailors to safety, he collapsed to the sand himself, mourning the man he couldn't save. Rising to his feet, he safely crossed the rest of the sand and approached the rock wall.

A huge barrier with a design that looked like the Sword of Light blocked the wall of stone. Cato pressed the huge sword against the barrier, but it wouldn't budge.

"Let there be light!" he cried, and the sword shone brightly. The light was exactly what they needed, and the barrier sank into the sand, revealing a deep tomb that receded into the rock for thousands of feet. Only a pale yellow circle reflected from the back wall, and Cato marveled at how long it must have taken to build this cavernous tomb.

A great ruby-covered spear shone back at them from the depths of the tomb, and this was what they sought.

Alzena noticed a scroll lying by the spear. She rolled it open and gasped in surprise. "It has some ancient writing on it in a different tongue, but I can translate it."

"What does it say?"

"Here lies the Bane of the Dragons. Tursas cursed me to live and die as a dragon, but I was once a great warrior. This weapon I have created is the only thing that will stop the black dragon forever. Take this spear and make sure it does not miss the dragon's heart. He needs to pay for what he did. These dragons were not always violent. They had their own realm here in Santara, and not too long ago they were even friends with the royalty. But then Tursas came and twisted the dragons. They went from being protectors to destructive menaces. Bring the reign of Tursas to an end, and my heart will finally rest. The rest is darkness. The rest is darkness."

Alzena placed the scroll back on the tomb.

Cato picked up the legendary Bane of the Dragons, securing the mighty weapon behind his back, and retreated.

They walked back away from the tomb, but were stopped by the broken bridge. Ilmatar knew that none of them could make it across the chasm on their own.

She opened her mind and communicated with Ukko. "Please hurry," she told him. "We're trapped in the Land of the Dead, in the Graveyard of the Dragons. I know you said you can't come in here, but if you can find a way to bend the rules, your little sister would really appreciate it!"

Cato began to pace before the bridge, being careful to avoid the quicksand now that he knew where it lay hidden.

"The bridge is ruined," said Cato. "Now what are we going to do?"

Ilmatar smiled. "Just keep calm, Cato. Help is on the way."

After a few minutes of watching Cato pace, Ilmatar finally saw the gigantic beard of Ukko begin to stretch down the corridors.

"There! I told you help was on the way!"

Cato waited until the beard fibers were within reach.

"Jump!" cried Cato. "Start climbing!"

As they pulled themselves up through the thick, rope-like strands of hair, Ukko's beard slowly retracted until they were passing safely over the graveyard. As they passed, though, Ukko's beard began to get very hot.

Fire raced through the cavern, dangerously close to the retreating beard, and Cato recognized the roar of the black dragon growing louder.

The fire-breathing dragon advanced through the cavern and sent another torrent of flame at Cato and his friends. It narrowly missed them, and the beard continued to get hotter, absorbing the heat.

"Hurry!" cried Cato.

"His face is miles away, he can't hear you," Ilmatar said.

Cato scowled in impatience. As he clung to the fibers, the heat became overwhelming. He shook his head violently as his hands began to singe and sizzle.

They finally reached the shore, and Cato cried, "Jump!" All the surviving sailors jumped at once, with Alzena and Cato and Ilmatar following close behind.

They managed to dive behind some rocks before the next blast from the black dragon sent a wall of flame across the sand. The rocks absorbed the fire, and it whooshed over their heads as they crouched behind them.

The rock quickly glowed red hot. Alzena's arm had been touching it and she pulled her arm away, trying to suppress a shout as she avoided burning her skin.

The flames disappeared above their heads, and Cato rose first, using the Sword of Light to send a blinding ray of light across the cavern directly into the dragon's red eyes. The brilliant beam blinded the dragon, which screamed and landed on the floor, covering its eyes with its front legs.

Cato took advantage of the moment to wield his massive spear and race across the sand to the blinded monster. Rather than throw the spear, he kept running with it, as the dragon fended off light arrows and tried to escape. Turning away, it tried to rescue itself and abandon the fight.

"Hey!" yelled Cato.

Even though the dragon was blind, it was far from deaf.

He plunged the spear all the way through its heart, and the dragon screamed hideously before it died. Ilmatar rushed over to the dragon, crying. Cato retrieved the heavy spear and compelled it back to its lighter shape.

"No! That's my daughter! You promised you wouldn't kill her."

As Ilmatar cried, she never lost her gaze on the dragon's face. The eyes opened slowly and this time, they were blue, like her baby girl's eyes, blue like the sea.

"Mother?" it said, looking up.

"Yes, daughter, I'm here. You're safe now."

The dragon closed its eyes again, and began to disintegrate, leaving only a blue-skinned goddess lying on the floor. Fully grown in the short weeks since Ilmatar had begun her quest, the goddess Loviatar opened her eyes and arose. The scales on her body were shining, even in the dim light of the cavern.

"We need to get out of here, Mother."

As the goddess stepped closer, the massive scales began to crack from her skin and peel away towards the sand. "We need to get her in the ocean now!"

Cato noticed that the beard was still hovering near them in the cavern.

"Let's get out of here right now!" said Cato. "We can fight Tursas later!"

"You don't have to worry about that. I promise you we'll come back!"

"No time to chat! Go!"

They ascended to Ukko's massive beard.

"We don't have much time. Tell him to hurry!"

They pulled slowly away from the Land of the Dead, the light getting brighter and brighter as they approached the exit.

The portal had weakened, for as they left the Land of the Dead and escaped into the wide-open ocean, none of them lost consciousness while they passed through.

Loviatar dove into the water, and Ilmatar dove in as well, but as Loviatar returned to the ocean, her blue scales were refreshed. Her arms and legs grew longer and began to flesh out as the ocean restored the goddess to her true power.

The massive Sea Goddess roared, to match that created by the black dragon.

Tursas exploded out of the portal, furious and raging. Cato looked up at the sky and devised a plan. "Ice arrows!" he screamed.

There was no chance for Tursas to move. The ice arrows formed instantly, and as Cato aimed the mighty bow, Ilmatar and her daughter forced billows of water through the air, arcing back down to the sea over Tursas. As the wall of water was consuming Tursas, Cato slammed arrows into Tursas and the water, causing the water to turn into solid ice.

Cato scrambled out of the cold water and onto the ice sheet. Once he got to his feet, he pulled the massive spear from his back. His foresight proved to be his advantage, because even though Tursas was trapped in the ice, the wizard was busily surging with fire and rage and melting it. Cato knew he didn't have much time and raced across the frozen surface as fast as he could. When he reached the wall of ice enclosing Tursas, it cracked into big pieces. Cato had to jump across the open water to shove the spear into the ice. It smashed the pieces apart, burying itself into Tursas's heart.

The flames died away and Tursas sank into the ocean, the ice breaking up and floating away. The powerful Sea Goddess swooped out of the sea and soared through the sky.

Chapter Twenty-Seven

After the battle ended and life returned to normal, Ilmatar recalled the ancient prisoners. She looked at Alzena beside her and asked, "What about Milla and Andri? They are the rightful owners of Tuonela, but they are still prisoners."

Alzena looked back at her. "Maybe we should free them then."

Loviatar waited while they all climbed up on her back. Fully grown, she could support many more people than this. Loviatar wordlessly swam back to the portal, and the passage was far less painful now that Tursas had been defeated.

Once they left the long underground river, the party had to descend a long stone staircase to reach the cages far below. The stairs were treacherous, with many of the stones sloping towards the abyss, but in spite of the danger, they pressed on, desperate to save the prisoners.

In the great distance, Ilmatar could hear two faint heartbeats. She heard no others besides those around her and the two faint flutters in the distance.

"I can hear their hearts! They are still alive, but barely."

Loviatar stepped back as a stone slipped out beneath her leg and plummeted to the abyss below.

"Get on my back!" said Loviatar. "It's getting too dangerous to travel on foot. Let me help you."

They all got on Loviatar's back again, and she took to the air and swooped down the steep staircase. Even though the sides became narrow and steep, the goddess expertly avoided the walls and made her way to the bottom of the staircase, where all of Tursas's prisoners were held.

She was horrified to see that Milla and Andri were still holding hands where the cages had been pushed together, their bodies limp and nearly lifeless. Milla and Andri looked like they were on the brink of death, ragged breaths rattling as the air escaped exhausted ribcages, their ribs nearly poking through the skin. They both lay on the rocks, struggling for breath, stubbornly holding onto each other's hands.

Cato rushed over at once and smashed the cages with his sword, bringing the ancient bars crashing to the ground.

Alzena and Ilmatar carefully moved the couple to a spot where the rock had been flattened by centuries of rituals.

They lay next to each other, and Andri opened her eyes, gazing in wonder at the empty space with no bars between her and her husband. She used her failing strength to bring her hand into a grasp with Milla's, collapsing into unconsciousness.

Loviatar quietly rose above Andri and gently spoke to her. "I'm going to heal you. You're going to be fine."

With her last strength, Andri opened her eyes long enough to show her awareness, and promptly fell asleep again, exhausted.

"Stand back," said Loviatar. "My powers are newly formed. I don't know exactly what will happen." She touched Andri with her healing hands. Sparkling white light spread out from her fingertips and covered the woman's body in glistening white light, working its way into her pores and healing her.

Her once-sunken body was now blossoming with new life. Her skin had been paper-thin and ancient, but as she was healed, the skin slowly transformed to a healthy white, large blue veins pumping underneath.

Milla's body was starting to come back to life, as well, strong blood welling up in his hand, then rushing into his arms and legs, and his powerful muscles began to grow back. Healthy skin began to replace faded, withered skin the texture of paper until his body was restored as well.

"That's amazing," whispered Loviatar. "I didn't even touch him. She was just holding hands with him."

Only Cato had the words to express what they were feeling as they gazed at the miracle. "That's the power of love," he declared, and nobody dared to question him.

As Andri awoke to her new body, a deep rush of air sucked into her lungs, and the resulting moan echoed off the cavern walls.

Ilmatar and Alzena were both stunned and approached the couple as soon as Loviatar became self-conscious and started backing away from the ancient rulers out of respect.

In response, Milla and Andri looked at one another and lowered their heads in respect.

"How can we ever repay you? You have given our lives and our kingdom back to us. We are forever in your debt. Who is this wise goddess who has healed us? We would repay her for the kindness."

Ilmatar smiled gratefully. "That is my daughter, Loviatar. She was the one who brought you and your wife back to your youth."

"Thank you, Loviatar," said Andri, smiling with youthful grace. "I owe you a tremendous debt. If you ever have need of us, Milla and I will be at your disposal whenever you ask." Her robes were still tattered, but with her youth restored, Andri had regained her regal presence, and her face had become hauntingly beautiful. "Tuonela used to be a solemn, stately realm where the dead rested, undisturbed. Now evil has left its mark. I have a lot of changes to make around here before things go back to normal." She gazed around the cavern with the cracked staircases and collapsing columns.

"I think we should leave you to your work, then," Cato said. Everyone in the party was more than happy to ascend to Loviatar's back. As they flew away back to Santara, the only head that turned back was Ilmatar's, so she could witness the dark red tendrils of magic emerge from Andri's and Milla's hands as they slowly began to heal the damaged realm.

Chapter Twenty-Eight

The evil creature that had been a Musaat tore through the forces defending her sisters. She had been driving through the soldiers for hours, but bringing down each opponent seemed to take an eternity. They fought back viciously, trained to protect the Musaat from any threat.

She wanted to reach her destination of the towers where her sisters were hiding, but the soldiers kept getting in the way.

She was about to get through the door of the tower when something stopped her in her tracks, a strange feeling deep inside as the curse that had been laid upon her began to falter and its power over her mind began to crack. Struggling to open the door, another wave of energy passed over her, and she tumbled to the ground.

Inside, the Musaat said, "Let me open the door!"

"It's not safe!" cried the guard.

"But that could be my sister outside. I'd know her voice anywhere."

"No! Don't open the door!"

"Or what?" asked the possessed Musaat.

The guard stepped back, afraid of what she would do to him.

She opened the door and recognized her sister's eyes immediately, even though the body was horribly disfigured. The curse began to lift and the first thing to return was her ice blue eyes. The Muse smiled with joy, although the guard was still confused and the people behind her were still ready to attack.

They waited for the creature to attack the Musaat first. It simply stood there, not moving, and so they did not advance.

The creature felt a strange snapping sensation deep inside her soul. She stopped fighting and started worrying, and felt the presence of Tursas fade away as his heart stopped. Once Tursas's heart had stopped beating, the curse was lifted, and her fractured skin slowly turned to darkness and flaked away, leaving the true Musaat exposed below.

Removed from the spell and returned to her divine form, Calliope looked at all the bodies around her and quietly held up her hands. "Can you ever forgive me?" she sobbed. "If I had captured you, you would have become another of Tursas's servants."

"You were under his control, dear sister. I know there's nothing you could have done. But now that he's gone, it's good to see you again."

Calliope smiled gratefully and replied, "It's great to see you too, sister."

Chapter Twenty-Nine

Ilmatar stood on the beach with Loviatar, the same beach where she had crawled ashore so many weeks ago, while all her new friends looked on.

"Ukko, hear my cry," she intoned. "Bring me back together with my Divine self. Let me become a Sky Goddess again."

Ukko emerged from the nebula, bringing his staff down to the water's edge.

"I'm sorry, but I have to go away now," Ilmatar said. "I don't want to hurt any of you." She removed her cloak and walked into the ocean, tall and proud. As she entered, she swam away from the shore.

Ukko brought forth powerful magic, and the staff began to glimmer. Sparkles poured from it and floated down to the water, covering Ilmatar in shimmering magic.

As the magic took effect, Ilmatar felt herself growing larger and larger, and looking down at her skin, she saw it changing to the thick skin of the goddess. The stretching of her bones as she grew was excruciating, and she remained submerged so the people on shore would not have to see her pain.

Ilmatar knew when her transformation was complete because the pain stopped and the magic flowed through her body as it had before.

She rose from the ocean, a great goddess from the depths. The water poured away from her body. Cato and the others on shore watched as this massive goddess rose from the ocean foot by foot until her entire body towered above them, wrapped in flowing robes the color of seafoam. They looked up at her, then bowed their heads in prayer.

Ilmatar hovered above the water, a powerful ruler of the sky once again.

She opened her hands wide and magic began to flow through them, as it once had. Baskets full of live fish, fresh for the cooking, and bushels of fresh fruit began floating down to the people on the shore.

"I told you I would reward you for your kind deeds, didn't I? These are your rewards for helping me, along with my eternal blessing."

As the baskets floated down, Loviatar took a deep breath and blessed the baskets and bushels with more magic.

Ilmatar turned to the great flying creature beside her.

"What was that magic for?" she asked.

"They will find out soon enough," Loviatar answered.

When the baskets landed, Cato pulled many fresh fish out and handed them to Lena, who arranged them by the fire to prepare them. Other women stepped forward too, eager to help with the feasting.

When he had reached the bottom of the basket, Cato turned around to start helping others, but a chorus of cheers and pointed fingers made him turn around. He gasped with astonishment as he saw the basket completely full of flopping, gasping fish again.

Ilmatar looked at Loviatar again. "That's what your magic was for? Neverending food?"

Loviatar grinned and chuckled.

Ukko laughed loudly, and even from his great height, the winds still whipped up the waves on the ocean. "She's turned out just like you," he said, laughing again.

"With these gifts, the people of Santara will never go hungry again!" Cato stopped talking because everyone was cheering.

Ilmatar rose high above the ocean, flying with Loviatar as they left the surface far behind. Loviatar looked around her new kingdom and smiled gratefully.

"This is the place where I rule," said Ilmatar. "Let's go to my castle. I need to make sure Ukko has been taking good care of it."

Ilmatar's palace floated deep in the nebula, nestled in clouds of her favored blue colors, and every tower still shone with the magic she had imbued in her sanctuary. The great palace remained unharmed, and Ilmatar breathed a sigh of relief that he hadn't damaged it.

Alzena declared that the Forbidden Forest should be forever renamed. Before a great crowd, she announced that the forest would now be called Ilmatar's Forest, and all the people of the kingdom were now welcome to return.

Chapter Thirty

After Calliope was returned to her true form, the other Musaat asked her to come to a meeting with them, and Calliope accepted gratefully.

When they got to the meeting, however, Euterpe had a very concerned look on her face, and Calliope knew something was not right

"Are you okay?" asked Euterpe. "Did he ever take you over completely?"

Although Musaat were never supposed to lie, Calliope insisted, "No, he never took over me completely. I had just enough strength to get here before I collapsed at the towers. Why?"

"When you got here, you were a monster. Don't you remember attacking the guards?"

"I don't remember that part at all. But you've never lied to me, so it must be so."

"What were you doing when he took you away?"

"They dragged me to the caves of Tuonela, but after I got there, I escaped the weak cage they trapped me in. I tried to hide in the deepest recesses of the cave, but somehow he found me and dragged me out."

Urania held up her hand to speak. Calliope fell silent. "You know the cardinal rule—the Musaat can never be seen. But the evil Tursas saw you when you were hiding in the cave, so you must have been revealing yourself somehow. And there's something else I'm confused about. When you were down there in the crowd, what were you doing in the first place? Why did you get seen?"

"I was just helping people be creative. Isn't that what we all try to do?"

"Calliope, the rules are there for a reason. Every time these humans come in contact with us, we lose a little of our divinity. Something inside us is weakened."

"I do feel not as strong as I used to be, but I don't feel compromised or damaged, if that's what you mean."

Euterpe gave her another worried look. "That's exactly what we're talking about. You haven't been yourself. You've been seen in public, and it's led to disastrous results. The monster that you became would have killed us if Cato hadn't won the battle with Tursas."

Calliope looked down at the table, and then glanced up and addressed her sisters with tears in her eyes. "I never meant to sound defensive, dear sisters. I am so sorry that I put you all in danger, but I promise you, as a Musaat, that I will never jeopardize our divine powers again."

Euterpe nodded her head peacefully, and Calliope exhaled deeply.

"We only want the best for you, divine sister. We wouldn't be talking to you if we weren't concerned. But you've squashed our doubts, and I think we should get back to work on rebuilding the city. We have so much work to do, helping the builders make this city what it used to be. In fact, I think we should help the builders improve the city, so that the stage roofs don't collapse anymore. We don't want another disaster on our hands."

The Musaat quietly filed out of the meeting hall and back to their towers. As Euterpe left, she took one last look at Calliope, and noticed a strange smirk on her face. Musaat weren't supposed to take any pride, but instead remain humble and flowing, so they could better inspire their subjects.

Euterpe paused before leaving, wondering if she should say something to Calliope. Then she saw an evil glint in her eye, a glint that faded a second later, making her wonder if she had ever seen it in the first place, but also unsettling enough to make her turn her back and leave the meeting hall without wasting another second.

About the Author

Melissa Saari

Melissa Saari lives in Washington State where the Columbia River, the river that powers America, rushes near her front door, and every summer, smoke from forest fires fill the sky. These powerful elements inspire her writing, whether it's romance, fantasy, or horror.

Melissa also has two loving, protective dogs: a female pit bull named Marla and a male Chow called Leo. Her dogs provide comedy, therapy, and inspiration for her stories.

Melissa will always be a writer. She begins her Master's Degree in Screenwriting this fall to study the complex film industry and how her vision can be shared with billions of moviegoers.

www.ingramcontent.com/pod-product-compliance
Lightning Source LLC
Chambersburg PA
CBHW030543130626
46552CB00006B/2404